T0209371

# Amazing Holiday Paws

## KAREN PETIT

WESTBOW
PRESS®
A DIVISION OF THOMAS NELSON
& ZONDERVAN

WestBow Press books may be ordered through booksellers or by contacting:

WestBow Press
A Division of Thomas Nelson & Zondervan
1663 Liberty Drive
Bloomington, IN 47403
www.westbowpress.com
1 (866) 928-1240

Scripture quotations are from the New Revised Standard Version Bible, copyright © 1989 the Division of Christian Education of the National Council of the Churches of Christ in the United States of America. Used by permission. All rights reserved.

ISBN: 978-1-9736-8612-5 (sc)
ISBN: 978-1-9736-8611-8 (hc)
ISBN: 978-1-9736-8613-2 (e)

Library of Congress Control Number: 2020902915

Print information available on the last page.

WestBow Press rev. date: 03/11/2020

# Contents

# Preface

Poetry's multimodal elements are described and illustrated in both of Dr. Karen Petit's books of poetry: *Amazing Holiday Paws* and *Holidays Amaze.* Petit's first published book of poetry, *Holidays Amaze,* has a preface that describes poetry as including visual and aural multimodal components: "Images are often 'seen' in the metaphors, similes, symbolic elements, format, sentence structures, use of icons, and the structure of a poem. Aural elements are hearable through the rhythms, rhymes, alliteration, and other sound elements."[1] Multimodal components also appear in *Amazing Holiday Paws,* Petit's second book of poetry. The poem "Multimodal Poetry on World Poetry Day (March 21)" and the maze version of this poem both have examples of visual and aural elements.

In addition to multimodal components, Petit's books of poetry include holiday content. The holiday settings in *Amazing Holiday Paws* enhance the connections within our lives. Holidays can connect us to pets, other animals, acquaintances, loved ones, personal history, our nation's history, the world's history, and religious history. In *Amazing Holiday Paws,* some of the holiday settings happen in Washington, D.C. The capital of the United States has many museums, statues, and other items to help people remember historic events. Holidays can help us all to create amazing memories based on our realities and history.

The holiday and Washington D.C. settings in *Amazing Holiday Paws* are enhanced with different viewpoints. With differing views and sometimes debate, the characters in this book of poetry can be people, animals, and/or dream versions of people and animals. For example, in the poem "Political Scratches from D.C.'s Dreaming Cat on National Cat Day," the D.C. Cat and a politician debate each other's views. While happening in Washington, D.C., the actions also happen as a part of the cat's view within its dream, so the readers can see what the cat is thinking about the politician. Some of the poems use capital letters to reference animals and small letters to reference people. These poems are partially showing the importance of the viewpoints of animals. Other poems have names for animals and/or names for people. Capitalization and/or names can illustrate the importance of a life.

The joy of knowing the animals in our world is the focus for *Amazing Holiday Paws*. People and animals often march together through life's mazes while using their feet and their paws. An animal's paws can be as strong as a person's feet and hands combined. Many animals can also see, smell, and clean their own paws. The cover design and the title of *Amazing Holiday Paws* both illustrate an animal's viewpoint about the importance of its paws.

People and animals often connect to each other with pats, loving rubs, visual analysis, and noises. *Amazing Holiday Paws* has some poetry that references the musical nature of animal sounds. A focus on animals can thus result in even more multimodal elements to help us dance to the music of our hearts, our souls, and our worlds.

# Acknowledgements

My family has always been loving and helpful. My thanks go to my children (Chris and Cathy), to my brothers and sisters (Ray, Rick, Margaret, Carl, Sam, Bill, Dan, and Anne), and to my nieces, nephews, cousins, and other relatives. Especially on the holidays, I love spending time with my family, their pets, and my cats.

I'm also very thankful for support from my many friends and colleagues at Phillips Memorial Baptist Church, the Community College of Rhode Island, Bristol Community College, Bryant University, Massasoit Community College, New England Institute of Technology, Quinsigamond Community College, Rhode Island College, Roger Williams University, the University of Massachusetts at Dartmouth, the University of Rhode Island, Worcester State University, and the Association of Rhode Island Authors.

WestBow Press has been helpful to many Christian authors. I have very much enjoyed their support. While the publication process can be a maze, it's also an amazing maze that has allowed my lifetime dream of being a published author to become my reality.

I am most thankful to God, Jesus Christ, and the Holy Spirit for my life, our world, and the many animals within our amazing world. I also love being a sheep who can follow an amazing shepherd. With God's help, the mazes of life are always amazing with the many paws encountered on its pathways.

# Illustrations

A Ferret Fast at Ferreting Solutions

# A Maze Poem: Ferrets Ferreting New Year's Resolutions (January 1)

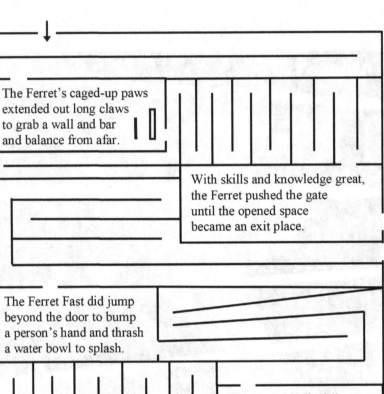

The Ferret's caged-up paws
extended out long claws
to grab a wall and bar
and balance from afar.

With skills and knowledge great,
the Ferret pushed the gate
until the opened space
became an exit place.

The Ferret Fast did jump
beyond the door to bump
a person's hand and thrash
a water bowl to splash.

The water all did fall
upon the floor to stall
the person's motions, so
more pets could exit slow.

The other ferrets ran
out of the cage to plan
some ferret games to play
with hands and toys that day.

To ferret out more maze,
all ferrets turn the page.

The human's hands reached down
with a towel to the ground;
with a soft cotton tool,
they dried the water's pool.

The ferrets Fast and slow
were fat enough to know
to move near hands and feet
if they wanted treats to eat.

The Ferret Fast did start
to bite a hand as a part
of demanding from the man
treats to start its game plan.

The Ferret Fast bit wrong
by biting way too strong,
instead of nipping sweet
on human hands to entreat.

The person yelled out "No!"
to make it run with woe
and teach it how to play
correct on New Year's Day.

The Ferret Fast now slid
to be with toys all hid
under the couch's frame
during a prior game.

The toys were hidden by
the ferrets on the sly
while playing many games
and planning New Year's aims.

The Ferret Fast was scared,
but soon peeked out and stared
at feet and paws resolved
to help make problems solved.

To ferret out more maze,
paws turn in diverse ways.

The other ferrets slow
were trained and both did know
to softly nip at hands
and not to bite demands.

The two slow ferrets showed
the Ferret Fast a road
to softly nip at hands
and follow all commands.

With playful chirping sounds,
both ferrets showed some bounds
of sweet and strong for bites
while acting out some fights.

Their first fight had tough jaws
pushing their teeth and claws
into teeth-cleaning toys
while making angry noise.

Their second fight was war
to save each other's core,
and Ferret knew their aim
was playing a war-like game.

Their next act had sweet nips
that touched each other's lips
with rhythmic noises warm
and motions to conform.

The ferrets did more acts
with strong and sweet contacts
over and over to teach
Ferret to others outreach.

When ferrets pawed around
near Ferret Fast's close ground,
their language said to play
with us some more today.

To ferret out more maze,
ferrets play on holidays.

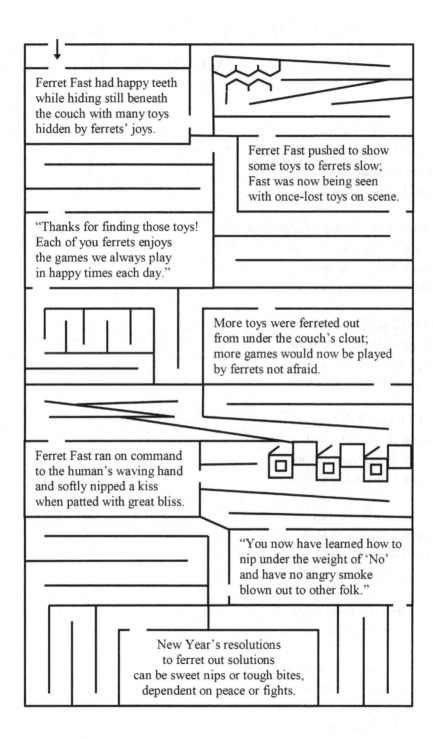

Ferret Fast had happy teeth
while hiding still beneath
the couch with many toys
hidden by ferrets' joys.

Ferret Fast pushed to show
some toys to ferrets slow;
Fast was now being seen
with once-lost toys on scene.

"Thanks for finding those toys!
Each of you ferrets enjoys
the games we always play
in happy times each day."

More toys were ferreted out
from under the couch's clout;
more games would now be played
by ferrets not afraid.

Ferret Fast ran on command
to the human's waving hand
and softly nipped a kiss
when patted with great bliss.

"You now have learned how to
nip under the weight of 'No'
and have no angry smoke
blown out to other folk."

New Year's resolutions
to ferret out solutions
can be sweet nips or tough bites,
dependent on peace or fights.

# Ferrets Ferreting New Year's Resolutions (January 1)

The Ferret's caged-up paws
extended out long claws
to grab a wall and bar
and balance from afar.

With skills and knowledge great,
the Ferret pushed the gate
until the opened space
became an exit place.

The Ferret Fast did jump
beyond the door to bump
a person's hand and thrash
a water bowl to splash.

The water all did fall
upon the floor to stall
the person's motions, so
more pets could exit slow.

The other ferrets ran
out of the cage to plan
some ferret games to play
with hands and toys that day.

To ferret out more maze,
all ferrets turn the page.

The human's hands reached down
with a towel to the ground;
with a soft cotton tool,
they dried the water's pool.

The ferrets Fast and slow
were fat enough to know
to move near hands and feet
if they wanted treats to eat.

The Ferret Fast did start
to bite a hand as a part
of demanding from the man
treats to start its game plan.

The Ferret Fast bit wrong
by biting way too strong,
instead of nipping sweet
on human hands to entreat.

The person yelled out "No!"
to make it run with woe
and teach it how to play
correct on New Year's Day.

The Ferret Fast now slid
to be with toys all hid
under the couch's frame
during a prior game.

The toys were hidden by
the ferrets on the sly
while playing many games
and planning New Year's aims.

The Ferret Fast was scared,
but soon peeked out and stared
at feet and paws resolved
to help make problems solved.

To ferret out more maze,
paws turn in diverse ways.

*Karen Petit*

The other ferrets slow
were trained and both did know
to softly nip at hands
and not to bite demands.

The two slow ferrets showed
the Ferret Fast a road
to softly nip at hands
and follow all commands.

With playful chirping sounds,
both ferrets showed some bounds
of sweet and strong for bites
while acting out some fights.

Their first fight had tough jaws
pushing their teeth and claws
into teeth-cleaning toys
while making angry noise.

Their second fight was war
to save each other's core,
and Ferret knew their aim
was playing a war-like game.

Their next act had sweet nips
that touched each other's lips
with rhythmic noises warm
and motions to conform.

The ferrets did more acts
with strong and sweet contacts
over and over to teach
Ferret to others outreach.

When ferrets pawed around
near Ferret Fast's close ground,
their language said to play
with us some more today.

To ferret out more maze,
ferrets play on holidays.

Ferret Fast had happy teeth
while hiding still beneath
the couch with many toys
hidden by ferrets' joys.

Ferret Fast pushed to show
some toys to ferrets slow;
Fast was now being seen
with once-lost toys on scene.

"Thanks for finding those toys!
Each of you ferrets enjoys
the games we always play
in happy times each day."

More toys were ferreted out
from under the couch's clout;
more games would now be played
by ferrets not afraid.

Ferret Fast ran on command
to the human's waving hand
and softly nipped a kiss
when patted with great bliss.

"You now have learned how to
nip under the weight of 'No'
and have no angry smoke
blown out to other folk."

*Karen Petit*

New Year's resolutions
to ferret out solutions
can be sweet nips or tough bites,
dependent on peace or fights.

An Innocent Squirrel

# Justice on Martin Luther King, Jr. Day (Third Monday of January)

The court house for justice stood strong and tall
upon a giant parking lot for all.
Parkers liked to engage in competition
to find and take the best parking position.

Up front, a single empty space was free,
and those who could take a long walking spree
would choose to use the back of the court's lot,
which displayed more than one empty parking spot.

Two cars at once did enter into the lot;
they both moved quickly toward the empty spot
that was closest to the entrance of the court
and near some bushes with nature's support.

With twenty feet to go to reach the spot,
each driver knew to quickly speed a lot
in order to be first to just arrive
before the other one could win and thrive.

The white car north of the spot swerved outward
with the intent of quickly turning inward
into the empty space that was waiting for
a speeding car to stop and park in its core.

The black car south of the space tried to glide
close to the line of cars on its left side
with the intent of blocking the empty spot
before it was seized by the turning white car.

The drivers became angry when they both
had to stop their cars; then began the growth
of negative words flying back and forth
and landing loudly between cars south and north.

The horns of both cars began to beep too much.
Three squirrels feared that someone would their space touch.
The three animals moved away from their bush
and chattered a lot while stamping their paws.

The black and white car owners both did see
the squirrels jumping really fast to flee;
the squirrels ran into the empty spot
while chattering still to each other a lot.

The noises from three squirrels unifying
did touch the hearts of car owners now sighing
about the space no longer being free,
but rather needed more by the squirrels three.

The owners turned off the engines of their cars
and walked forward to view the squirrels as stars;
their cell phones took pictures and flashed with lights,
which forced the squirrels to move with no insights.

Under rows of cars, the squirrels did run
without watching for movements from anyone
who might be a danger blocking their way
to a safer place where they could briefly stay.

In the back of the parking lot's many rows,
one of the three running squirrels bumped its nose
against a tire on a slowly moving van;
the two other squirrels paused and then ran.

The two squirrels stopped running next to a tree;
they turned to view their injured friend to see

what was happening between him and the van:
the van's door opened, and out stepped a man.

The man locked up his van and glanced quickly
at the injured squirrel that was thickly
covered by its fur while it lay on the ground
in shock without moving or making a sound.

The black and white cars drove close to the van
and parked in empty spots before drivers ran
over to the squirrel that seemed asleep
upon the ground between the van and a jeep.

The man who owned the van asked the car owners:
"Why were you fighting for space like landowners
when you were both parking in a public space
that's empty now near the entry to this place?"

The black and white car owners both seemed mad
at each other as one of them said, "We're sad!
We made all of those cute squirrels run,
and neither one of us has that great space won!"

"You don't look like you're sad; you rather look mad;
now look back at that spot; there's a person glad
that both of you left a good spot up there free,
so he or she can next to the entrance be."

The white and black car owners both looked back
to where they'd been mad enough to attack
each other when they both wanted the same thing:
a good place to be to avoid some walking.

The empty space was filled with a red car;
a wheelchair person had won the parking war
and was visible now to people and cops
who would enter the building for legal stops.

The car owners' faces really appeared sad
as they looked at each other and felt bad
about their stressed-out actions noticed by all
and three squirrels that wanted to away crawl.

One of the car owners softly did say,
"I'm so sorry for what I did today.
I was anxious and stressed by other traffic
that was so bad it was photographic."

The other car owner smiled and shook her head
in agreement before she waved her phone and said,
"These days, no one can ever be perfect,
especially on roads with cameras and traffic."

The van owner frowned in disagreement;
"I'm worse, since I hit a squirrel innocent.
He doesn't even seem to be alive,
but I'll see if I can help him to survive."

The van owner walked toward the squirrel's form
as a car owner said, "We should keep him warm.
Even with all of his heavy fluffy fur,
my coat's extra warmth might be what he'd prefer."

Before the car owner took off her coat,
the van owner was touching the squirrel's throat
to see if the animal was still alive
and possibly able to be healed and thrive.

The squirrel suddenly awoke and ran free
to join the squirrels right next to the tree;
they used their paws like they were wearing boots
to run under bushes and over large roots.

The squirrels all looked happy and healthy
as they ran near cars in a manner stealthy

before moving into a garden area
while they all displayed far less hysteria.

Upon some grass away from cars in the street,
the three squirrels all paused together to eat;
the injured one's nose appeared unbeaten
and able to smell the food being eaten.

The people had stopped being able to see
the actions of squirrels that now were free
to live better lives because justice had turned
to help with the freedom for all concerned.

A car owner gazed all around while she said,
"I think that squirrel's okay and not dead.
You hit it because it was running fast
to get away from our noises so vast."

The van owner smiled to show his agreement.
"I guess we often have anger to vent;
we should all try to be more peaceful and pray
to stay thankful, so things will work out okay."

One owner checked her watch to see her delay;
"I'm okay, but are we really all okay?
Do either one of you need to be in court
right away to avoid a prison transport?"

The other car owner said, "I'm really fine.
I'm just out here to help a friend of mine.
She needs emotional support from friends
who'll sit and watch while she tries to make amends."

The owner who had checked her watch was aghast;
"Oh, you really do need to get in there fast;
if I had known you needed to help a friend,
my actions while parking, I would now amend."

"I'm here a little bit early anyway;
my friend will have family there today;
while waiting for me, she'll be fine and well,
especially when she hears about that squirrel."

"I'm glad your friend has help to make her stronger.
I'm okay out here, too, for a bit longer.
I just need to pick up some papers and fudge
from my lawyer after she's heard from the judge."

The other car owner now checked the time past
on her cell phone, laughed, looked hungry, and asked,
"Is your lawyer really giving you candy?
How much extra does she charge, or is it free?"

"It's free and sweet to have within my life
so many connections to reduce my strife
during new events after a war happens
between differing views and newer trends."

The van owner said with a laughing cough:
"Sometime today, I just need to drop off
all this paperwork for my lawyer to use.
He'll be in there for me any time I choose."

The car and van owners all walked together
into the court house with perfect weather
to help to heal each future injury
and make all in the world even more free.

Justice works the best in a true democracy
when all interact, connect, and still are free
to address the problems and errors in life
with more helpfulness and less anger and strife.

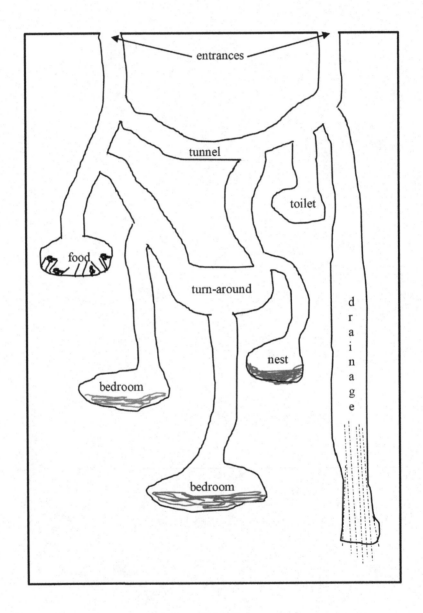

A Groundhog's Burrow

# Climate Change on Groundhog Day (February 2)

⁓✖⁓

The second month began its second day
with Philly seeing light from morning's glow;
he left his burrow's entrance right away
and saw his shadow's scary climatic show.

His shadow stretched too big in front of him
until it bumped against other shadows
that tumbled down from a tree's storming limb
to smash into Philly's sniffling nose.

The groundhog's shadow itself did eject
away from Philly while weathering storms
and becoming scared to try to deflect
the darker shadows of tree and limb forms.

When Philly's shadow slid its two front paws
within a tree's shadow that wasn't warm,
the shadowed paws lost the shape of their claws
in frozen shade that stretched out too far from the tree's wooden form.

Then Philly's shadow became super scared
and ran with Philly into his burrow
to hide from climate changes not repaired
and weather six more weeks of winter's snow.

On one of that winter's days, too quickly,
the snow did fall with temperatures warm;
even though still scared, the groundhog Philly
did peek outside to view a noisy storm.

The snow was heavier than in past storms
because the warm air was making wet snow
that moved with wind to make frozen forms
and slam an entrance to Philly's burrow.

After too many weeks of winter's snow,
a voice inside the humans' house then said,
"Our electricity again did go!
I'll run outside to cook our meat and bread!"

Another voice did say so soft and sweet:
"Our neighbors keep using fires to cook, too;
do you think we're all adding too much heat,
so the climate's becoming more askew?"

"One fire really cannot impact the world,
so we should just do what we have to do
to eat our food within our changing world
and let others do what they have to do!"

The end-of-winter fire did melt more snow,
resulting in water that kept flowing
into all the chambers of the burrow,
where Philly to his life and home did cling.

When spring appeared, the heat was stronger still.
With many yards flooded by too-much rain,
umbrellas were used for each outside grill,
so desires strong for heated food could reign.

Using his paws, Philly kept on digging
at water flooding into his burrow,
and experienced a thundering spring
with rain that rammed his mazing tunnels low.

A wave of heat then helped the water leave,
so plants could try to grow in dreadful soil

without nutrients to help them achieve
a life amid some fires that did them broil.

Most gardens withered due to burns from heat,
so Philly couldn't find his preferred food,
but insects and roots were all he could eat
because nearby yards did just them include.

Then summer's climate brought heaviest rain;
many storms of thundering noise and lights
did join each amiss-season hurricane
and make poor Philly swim for days and nights.

When Philly one day left his burrow to roam
and look for clover, dandelions, and grass;
he glanced up at the house above his home
to see people watching from windows' glass.

The house atop Philly's flooded burrow
was a small home for a family of four;
they often saw and smelled the smoke aglow
in each neighbor's yard with a fireplace roar.

The people living dry within their house
above the burrow's chambers and tunnels
talked to Philly like he was a large mouse
coping with changing climate's water swells.

"Are you sad to see our climate changing
with smoke and higher degrees Fahrenheit?
Your heated burrow's now water's plaything
and seems to have an ocean's rising height."

"You're the groundhog! Do your job correctly!
Don't just predict the climate! Fix it, Phil!"
The groundhog thought his true name was Philly,
and the people were trying to make him ill.

23

Since Philly now was scared of the yelled words,
he whistled to warn other animals
to run away and hide from foolish nerds
who wrongly were talking like radicals.

He madly watched the people light a fire
in their yard's fireplace, sprinkle some rain,
and create some heated wind with the fire,
followed by a level-six hurricane.

When fall arrived with storms and falling leaves,
more hurricanes appeared on land and sea;
the storms tore trees to fall down with their leaves
and damage the homes of people and Philly.

Many humans' houses had losses small
with water rising, increased wind, and heat.
Philly's home had damage to tunnels all,
no open exits, and no place to eat.

When stuck with watered mud in his burrow,
all Philly could do to breathe in some air
was to twist and turn the mud far below
to make it shift its space and let in air.

When Philly dug against a blocked exit,
after seven hours, he opened it up;
the grass and plants outside were still unfit
because fiery change had burned them up.

To look for some edible plants and grass,
Philly ran in yards that he didn't know
'til a fox in yards did also trespass;
then Philly ran back into his burrow.

People came out of their house by wind harmed,
looked at the three burrow holes remaining,

and stared at spots where plants used to be farmed;
these places now had not a living thing.

"Too many fires out here are bad for us,
and many others are suffering, too;
with not enough food for them and for us,
what else can people and animals do?"

"We can't even buy any more coffee!
Too many forests are burned or flooded,
so the cost's too high for coffee and tea!
Drinking just water is something I dread!"

"At least we always have water and bread,
and sometimes can buy other items for food;
in many countries, people are unfed
and would love to eat our bread barbecued."

"Animals are eating our food too much!
We can often not even eat poultry!
Animals steal our food and space too much!
Creating their own food their goal should be!"

"Animals are alive and need food, too;
we shouldn't from them ourselves separate,
but should once again have more than one zoo
to help them to live before it's too late."

"The groundhogs still living under our home
haven't moved like they're really supposed to!
They should now move to wooded spots and roam
around to create some burrows brand new!"

"Perhaps they just want to stay in our yard
because of the grass and weeds we once had,
or perusing other yards may be hard
to do without making some strangers mad."

"If we want to grow some more garden plants,
we'll need to scare all the groundhogs away!
Then we'll be able to eat some good plants
and not be as hungry every day!"

"With all the wind and floods and storming heat,
many animals in yards do trespass
before returning home with nothing to eat,
unable to find any weeds or grass."

When Philly heard the voices talking bad,
he twisted in his turn-around chamber
and licked soil from a paw drooping-down sad
while being too skinny in his chamber.

The loudest voice coughed twice before it said,
"We can't really change what we've been doing!
We'd all be healthier and better fed
if this changing climate wasn't storming!"

Even though Philly sneezed in his burrow,
no one heard him or saw his nervous paw
as he snuck out from the entrance to know
if what he was hearing was what he saw.

The softer voice had some breathing trouble
and then was able to talk while wheezing:
"If great spoken ideas had filled our mouths full,
years back, we still could not have changed a thing."

"You're right! The people back then loved to drive
their giant, super-fast, gas-powered cars!
They used too-much gas to quickly arrive
and added to our planet's cuts and scars!"

The tail of Philly moved to show its scars,
attained while fighting animals, shadows,

the climate, bikes, and small electric cars;
these made him often hide in his burrows.

When Philly realized all of the sounds
came from anti-climate burners talking,
he moved backwards while voicing his own sounds
and showing his fears of burrow blocking.

"The laws should have so required everyone
to use hybrid cars, buses, and subways,
as well as power from the wind and sun,
to save energy and improve our days!"

"I think some people really didn't know
about carbon and methane emissions;
the climate changes not too long ago
could have been fixed with better conditions."

"The people and companies too many
needed gas, oil, and coal, instead of none,
so things couldn't have been fixed completely,
but more improvement could still have been done!"

"We can help ourselves and animals now
while some are still alive in this mayhem
by sharing with others our space and chow,
instead of hungering and hurting them."

"We're more important than animals all
because we're smarter and can fix our Earth,
so climate changes can be made to stall
by giving new technologies their birth!"

"Extinct animals are now too many,
due to closed zoos, no food, and much disease;
even if we fixed the climate plenty,
we still couldn't fix the vanished species."

"We're all dying! We must think about this!"
Before the mouth could close its lips unkind,
a bee flew in, stinging the wetness amiss,
exited, and left no honey behind.

The paws of Philly strongly clapped in joy
about the bee's attack on climate change
done by people who wanted to destroy
the world with heated chemicals' exchange.

"The groundhogs have helped us to keep our home
when they changed that water to heavy mud
by digging holes for the water to roam
down into their burrows during that flood."

"That could have hurt the structure of our home,
which really is so wishy-washy now
that we'll soon fall and will then have to roam
in burrows beneath our home anyhow!"

"They didn't hurt—they helped our home largely
by keeping water out of our basement;
they also helped to keep us all healthy
by eating insects that could us torment."

"A second ago, a bee stung my tongue,
so now I'm talking in a bitten way!
The groundhogs instead should have all been stung
because of their eating no bees today!"

"Most bees are gone, and they can't make us sick.
The really big problem is mosquitoes,
which are making so many people sick.
The rising water has increased these woes."

"The groundhogs should eat the insects a lot,
so we don't have all these problems with bites!

Especially now when it is too hot,
we're bitten too much on too many nights!"

"Groundhogs are often too wobbly and weak
to help us by eating all of the insects;
we should give them a little food to tweak
their strength with nutrition's useful effects."

"The groundhogs are only just meaningless!
To give to them our food would be so wrong!
They have their food in the wild to access,
and our food has been rotten for so long!"

"Right now, we're really not super hungry
unlike the weak animals in our yard;
they're all so sick and scared and too skinny
as they run around, getting hurt and scarred."

"No extra food's in our cupboards for them!
We need to keep all of our food for ourselves!
We just can't even think of feeding them,
or we'll find hunger, not food, on our shelves!"

"What about that lettuce moldy and gray?
You now don't want to eat it anyway,
and we've talked about throwing it away;
we could simply toss it outside today."

"You're being smart about that rotting food!
We'll give that groundhog half of the lettuce
while watching him closely to see his mood!
If he likes the food, it'll be safe for us!"

The people walked inside as one did fuss;
a minute later, the soft-voiced person
came back out with a handful of lettuce
with no normal leaves—not a single one.

Near Philly's burrow, the lettuce was placed;
when Philly did smell his favorite food,
he paused until the person sweet had raced
back into the home with noises subdued.

Then Philly moved carefully through a tunnel
and twisted into the fastest pathway
that led straight up to the lettuce's smell
as he climbed up to his favorite doorway.

After grabbing a chunk of lettuce thin,
he stuffed it in his mouth while standing tall;
his teeth were showing, and his mouth did grin
as the taste and smell did his mind enthrall.

From inside the house, the people did see
that Philly was happy to eat his food.
The lettuce indoors looked so unhealthy,
but the people still chose to eat this food.

They ate while watching Philly finish his treat;
He then ran to his burrow four-feet deep
to enjoy more peaceful climatic heat
inside his chamber for his winter's sleep.

As hibernation entered Philly's life,
climatic change did some tunnels delete.
Creations did wither with weather's strife;
added problems happened with heightened heat.

*Abraham Lincoln,* Created by Daniel Chester French, 1920
Located in the Lincoln Memorial, National Mall, Washington, D.C.

# Backpack Freedom on Lincoln's Birthday (February 12)

The backpack enclosed its items unfree,
confined tightly while in Washington, D.C.
and approaching the Lincoln Memorial
without seeing monuments pictorial.

Within the heavy backpack filled to its brink
were pens enslaved with their black unwritten ink;
they were near folders with papers inside
that wanted to be seen and not to hide.

An anti-slave war began when the backpack
shifted to the South and made the zipper crack;
the owner tried to move it back to the North
while pausing to stop and not walking forth.

Some keys for the North and the South were dropped
when the owner and the backpack both stopped
with angry movements to fight to be free
in their own state, rather than united be.

The person was mad at the zipper's crack
and flung the full backpack off of his back,
only to have more items dropping free
and hitting his toe to gain their liberty.

Some parts of the backpack still full appeared
as cages holding items commandeered
and kept too deep within the backpack's space
without receiving wages for their place.

The owner kicked the zipper's fastened spot
and made the noise of a tiny gunshot
while breaking the metal, so it opened up
and forced emancipation to be set up.

Thirty-six papers flew into the air
with the "Thirteenth Amendment" written clear
in black ink upon each of the white pages
that flew from differently placed cages:

> Neither slavery nor involuntary servitude, except as a
> punishment for crime whereof the party shall have been
> duly convicted, shall exist within the United States, or any
> place subject to their jurisdiction.[2]

A breeze did unite the papers together,
so each did fly like an eagle's feather
up to the Lincoln Memorial's statue,
where each thanked Lincoln for what he did do.

As time progressed, the papers kept flying;
with more papers connecting and joining
their lawful journey to be a free nation
by stopping slavery and segregation.

The papers kept flying near the water cool
of the Lincoln Memorial Reflecting Pool;
the ducks and geese pushed all papers together
while free to swim with each webbed foot and feather.

The backpack's owner let papers and pens
move into his backpack as if they were friends,
but only the ones that wanted to be there
were stacked together with freedom to share.

The statue of Abraham Lincoln looked down
at the many visitors walking around;
the viewers of Lincoln's thoughtful hands and face
were friending others outside of their race.

Two Cat Brothers

# Cat Brothers on Valentine's Day (February 14)

Two cats each other did exclude
while staring at a bowl of food.
Since both did want to eat it first,
their eyes in battle then submersed.

They glared at one another to move
too close to make their spots improve;
they both did hiss their desire to eat
while edging close to the bowl of meat.

The larger cat was old and trained
to behave himself and be restrained;
his actions when under this day's stress,
were seen by others as regress.

The smaller cat was still too young
to stop its active hissing tongue
from moving fast to reach the food
and swatting others to not intrude.

Before the cats enhanced their fight,
the bowl was raised to a higher height
by the owner of the hissing cats;
she gave them both some loving pats.

With petted fur upon their backs,
the cats did change their eyes to relax;
since both still wanted the bowl of meat,
they rubbed against the owner's feet.

The owner grabbed a second bowl
to split the food as her main goal;
when she did place the bowls half-filled
upon the floor, the cats were thrilled.

The bowls were placed next to each other;
each cat could now act like a brother
and share some love while eating food
within a spot for a better mood.

The cats did eat their food in fun;
without a hiss from either one,
they switched between each other's bowls
and turned around to different roles.

The both took turns to be in charge,
and neither acted super large;
they licked the faces of each other
and shared each kiss like with a brother.

All pets are family members true,
who fight and love on days anew;
their paths are mazes intertwined
with paws that walk in lines entwined.

Washington Monument, National Mall, Washington, D.C.

George Washington Sculpture, created by Horatio Greenough, 1840
Located in the Smithsonian National Museum of
American History, Washington, D.C.

# An American Dream on Washington's Birthday (February 22)

About five hundred fifty-five feet tall,
the Washington Monument on the mall
reflected across the Reflecting Pool
to reach out to all of the people and pets in weather cool.

The extending reflection in winter's cold
stretched far beyond the circle of U.S. flags that refused to fold
amid the number of visitors agleam
with all their love for the American Dream.

In front of the Washington Monument
were circular sidewalks that seemed to be meant
to help each person walking with a pet
to love taking turns without feeling upset.

One owner of a dog walked a bit slowly
while texting info into her phone wholly
about George Washington's dogs helping with life
while under Revolutionary War's strife.

George Washington loved animals so much;
whenever possible, he stayed in touch
with different animals on many days
that became a part of his freedom maze.

In 1774, Sweet Lips,
one of Washington's sweetest dogs for trips,
was taken by Washington to assist
the Continental Congress to persist.

George Washington's horses did help him, too;
he rode on Nelson and Blueshin to pull through
the Revolutionary War's times of grief
while being a great Commander in Chief.

When one of British General Howe's dogs
trailed Americans like it was one of their dogs,
Commander-in-Chief Washington did order
the dog be sent back to its British owner.[3]

Such acts of kindness in Washington's life
helped others to feel a little less strife
and reflect on some more positive pools
to mirror their goals while making new rules.

To see the Washington Monument's a thrill.
Within the National Mall flows goodwill
through the pool images that can enthrall
all the visitors who pause to see this mall.

Visitors think of Washington's history
as a great president who led our country;
elected he was unanimously
for two terms within our democracy.

Inside the monument's obelisk form
stands a Washington statue in uniform
that's touching a sword, fasces, cane, and cape;
the plow behind suggests a farmer's landscape.

That day, the monument had visitors glad
about all of the freedom that they now had;
many smiled at their friends and at strangers, too,
as they explored pathways both old and new.

Some people walked across the mall to see
the Smithsonian's exhibits for free

43

with statues, works of art, and information
about our world, animals, and our nation.

Just inside the National Museum
of American History's a well-done
marble sculpture honoring George Washington
and showing some knowledge free for everyone:

> "The classically inspired sculpture honored Washington
> as a leader in war and peace—the victorious general who
> voluntarily handed his power, symbolized by the sword,
> back to the people."[4]

The reflecting pool in the National Mall
displayed many reflections both short and tall
from visitors moving in diverse ways
to walk through our country's historic maze.

The phone-holding dog owner was stepping round
without watching too high above the ground.
When another person walking fast came near,
the dog did pull the owner to sideways veer.

The visitor also stepped to the side
while asking about who was the leash's guide:
"Are you an owner who sometimes pulls that leash,
or is your dog always the puller of that leash?"

The dog owner looked at the visitor's head
and laughed at the too-tight scarf as she said,
"Even with leashes, we're both still happy,
due to Washington's actions to make us free."

"I guess that leash is just a connection
that joins you and your dog in one direction,
when you're both together and in a maze
of turns for feet and paws to love always."

"Even when this leash does not connect us,
our love and thoughts for each other are a plus
that keep us connected; whether we're near
or far apart, our closeness will give us cheer."

When the visitor stepped near the tiny dog
that was wagging its tail and jumping like a frog,
the dog was happy to have its love expand
and licked the visitor's extended hand.

"It's so strange seeing you pat my dog like that;
I once had a dream about pets not fat.
While most had come from different places,
a few were born within the center's spaces.
They all were living in a crowded center
with too many pets for people to enter.
Potential adopters were not let inside
and were stopped outside. Even when they tried
to adopt a pet right next to the door,
they were still denied a new pet to adore.
The creatures had scant food their stomachs to fill,
so the shelter's owners decided to kill
most of them, so some could be allowed to live
with small amounts of food that people might give.
Before the day for animals to sleep,
volunteers offered to foster and keep
all of the shelter's animals in their homes,
so none would die from problems or syndromes."

"I can't believe all animals were adopted.
Even in a dream, people must have opted
to not adopt the scratchers, barkers, chewers,
attackers, fighters, and other wrongdoers."

"Some foster families did adopt them all;
they really loved to save some lives, even small.
The wrongdoers were forgiven for their wrongs
and trained to be better pets to sing great songs.
My dog was present in my dream and jumping
with joy every time adopters were pausing
in their busy lives to pat, feed, and love him;
the dogs, people, and cats all barked a hymn."

"Those animals rescued and loved in your dream
illustrate living the American dream;
they had their homes, food, and chances to improve
their lives while working to help others improve."

"They really did live as part of freedom's glee
in their American dream's diplomacy
while interacting with people and creatures
to enhance many lives with many features."

The owner, dog, and visitor walked among
the Washington Monument's flags that sung
the American dream reality sweet
when amazing wind did sound for paws and feet.

Museum of the Bible, Washington, D.C.

# Choosing Photos On National Photo Day (Second Sunday of March)

The photos were shifting
within a plastic bin
while parents were driving
to their new house to move in.

The children, Stan and Nan,
as they kicked with their toes
at the bin in the van,
heard sounds from framed photos.

The photos filled each frame
with smiles for fancy fame
or frowns for worthless shame;
they then began their game.

To be on top would mean
a higher status spot,
some added light to glean,
and lessened risk to rot.

Wishing never to be
beneath some heavy frames
were pictures of family
and pets in diverse frames.

Each time the bin did shift,
most photos' frames were moved
within the stack adrift
to spaces unimproved.

The pets in photos sweet
did bump each other's frames
to try and others beat
and win their first of games.

The frame around a cat
did scratch a pictured dog
while begging for a pat
from photos near the dog.

The dog's response was barks
that sounded when his frame
did hit and make some marks
upon the cat's wood frame.

More frames all jumped around
inside the plastic bin
to snarl and bark with sound
within their space too thin.

Two photos of people
did pat their nearby pets;
their frames did push and pull
to rub their love to pets.

The scratches and the barks
then stopped their angry sounds
to purr and say remarks
while making loving sounds.

Now still within the van,
the children's shoeless feet
had no enclosing ban
to keep them clean and neat.

Their lively dirty toes
did kick above the bin

and drop some dirt to pose
with photos in the bin.

The photo on the top
within a real-gold frame
did shift enough to drop
the dirt for others' shame.

Within the golden frame
were painted gems on shoes,
and all the gems could claim
the shoes were theirs to choose.

The dirt fell downward fast
to harm the photos low;
within the pile so vast,
more harm did happen low.

The ugly injured ones
were lowest in the pile
and furthest from the sun's
bright skills to make them smile.

A wrinkled cardboard frame
enclosed a picture old
of feet with naked shame
for scratches, dirt, and mold.

The dirty frame encased
a pic of painted feet
that younger Nan first traced
as her artistic feat.

The frame and picture both
were cheaply planned and made
by someone trying growth
whose income low had stayed.

The dirty frame of feet
tried climbing up the pile
above the photos neat
that thought all dirt was vile.

When almost at the top
of frowning photos mad,
the dirty feet did stop
and paused while looking sad.

The gems in golden frame
atop the photo pile
were flashing forth their flame
of angry light to rile.

The cheap and dirty feet
did move up more to show
their strong work to compete
in the game of light and low.

The golden frame that backed
its richest gems with heat
attacked, attacked, attacked
and tried to hurt the feet.

The feet were scratched and hot,
but still did want the shoes
to share their high-up spot
and shade sun-burning views.

The golden frame with shoes
enough for photos all
with greed did just refuse
and pushed the feet to fall.

The dirty feet did fall
within their cardboard frame

while trying not to maul
the others in the game.

Both children looked to see
which photo frame would win
and be the first to be
removed from in the bin.

The most expensive frame
was still the highest one;
its smile about the game
did "say" that it had won.

The car did turn and stop;
the photos all did slide,
but those upon the top
did not go down the slide.

The photos low did try
to move atop the pile,
so they'd be seen most high
and chosen first to smile.

The few on top were strong
and kept their frames too high,
refusing to belong
with most below their sky.

Then Stan and Nan transferred
the bin of photos large
into their room preferred
right next to the garage.

As children both did stare
at shelves across the room,
one shelf had money's snare;
their eyes toward it did zoom.

The cash to them did mean
they'd give their friends a peek
at pay for helping clean
their other house last week.

The children slid the bin
as photos in the pile
did fight some more to win
and live the best lifestyle.

Nan's hand moved in the bin
and past the golden frame.
She chose it not to win,
which made it lose the game.

The golden frame attacked
the hand within the bin;
some angry scratches smacked
for choices made within.

The hand of Nan was brushed
by other photos sweet
that saw her face had blushed
to feel the scrapes not neat.

Some dirty dust did land
on frames and then fell down
upon Nan's scratched-up hand,
which seemed to form a frown.

Nan's eyes did view the ground
between her feet and Stan's.
To clean the photos' mound,
she used her dirty hands.

Some photos lost some dirt,
but some received more dust

as hands did shift the dirt
to intersperse with dust.

The naked-feet photo,
too low inside the pile,
got added dirt and woe
to make it seem more vile.

The hands of Stan and Nan
did both do shifting more
to follow their own plan
for choosing-their-pics chore.

Pics of friends from the stack
were picked up first of all
and placed upon the rack
near cash for their enthrall.

Stan used his phone to take
a picture of the shelf
and sent the pic to make
his friends as glad as self.

A friend did text him back:
"We're glad you have more pay.
We love that cash feedback
about our work today."

The hands of Stan and Nan
did move within the bin
to follow more their plan:
the pics of pets did win.

A parent grand arrived
to help arrange them all;
the photos really thrived
once placed upon the wall.

Some photos were arranged
to show the ancestry
through placements being changed
for pets' and people's glee.

The golden frame of shoes
was in the bin near feet,
was sad, and did refuse
to help the painted feet.

With hands still moving frames,
remaining pics desired
their preferred placement aims
be safely now acquired.

While seeing nothing there,
a hand did shove a pic
of Jesus Christ somewhere
below another pic(k).

This blessed Jesus photo
was taken to enable
historic religious glow:
Museum of the Bible.

Stan and Nan loved always
to recall museum trips
and to give Jesus praise
when they saw bible scripts.

Now, they were focused, though,
on other things around
and saw not the best photo
that was pushed too far down.

The picture of Christ fell far
below the other frames,

accepting each new scar
from others' dirty frames.

When hands moved photos fast,
the frames again did shift.
Christ's frame with scars too vast
was crowned with splinters swift.

The splintered photo's frame—
to help the other frames—
still played within the game,
so they'd have winning aims.

The dirty painting made
from Nan's once childish feet
did not move up but stayed
near splintered photo sweet.

Some light did shine with glee
to land upon Christ's painting,
attracting eyes to see
that Jesus was the king.

Christ's frame did sweetly land
on pictured feet of Nan;
it cleaned some dust so grand;
Nan's better life began.

Nan picked up, hugged, and kissed
the painting of her feet,
while looking like she'd missed
her childhood art so neat.

The photo then was placed
upon a shelf with room
for other pics erased
of sinful, dirty doom.

The shining light was lit
upon some other pics
to have their lives transmit
more hugs and fewer kicks.

The frame with gems did turn
to face the photo best
of Jesus and did learn
how to be spirit-blessed.

The golden-framed gem photo
did slide to where the feet
had been just seconds ago;
it wished to help the feet.

The newly-Christian frame
now showed its shoes as strong;
the hand of Stan just came
to make a right from wrong.

The shoes with gems were moved
behind the painted feet;
the shining gems improved
and glistened with the feet.

The glass on Christ's photo
reflected light from the bin
to give the room a glow
to be seen by all kin.

Seeing Christ in the photo
caused all to kneel in prayer;
the hands of Nan did know
to raise this pic(k) with care.

Christ's photo ascended
onto the highest shelf;

a golden light then spread
to every shelf and self.

The splinters and the scars
in the frame of Christ's photo
became historic memoirs
as they vanished in the glow.

All eyes stayed upwards toward
the highest photo's light,
which made all frames on board
be spots of new delight.

All photos won the game
by worshipping Christ's name
and loving His acclaim
that lighted every frame.

# A Maze Poem: Multimodal Poetry on World Poetry Day (March 21)

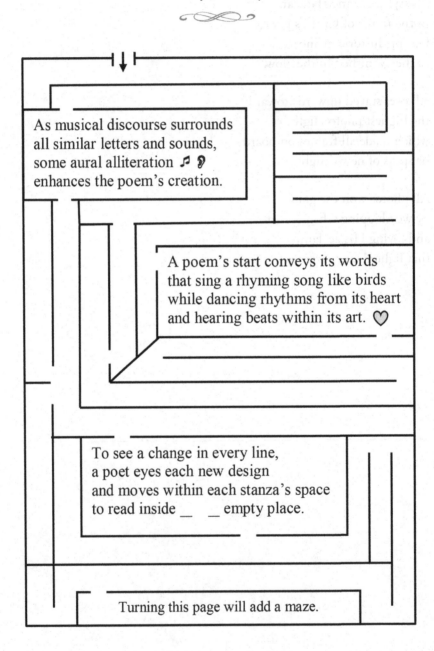

As musical discourse surrounds
all similar letters and sounds,
some aural alliteration ♪ ♫
enhances the poem's creation.

A poem's start conveys its words
that sing a rhyming song like birds
while dancing rhythms from its heart
and hearing beats within its art. ♡

To see a change in every line,
a poet eyes each new design
and moves within each stanza's space
to read inside __ __ empty place.

Turning this page will add a maze.

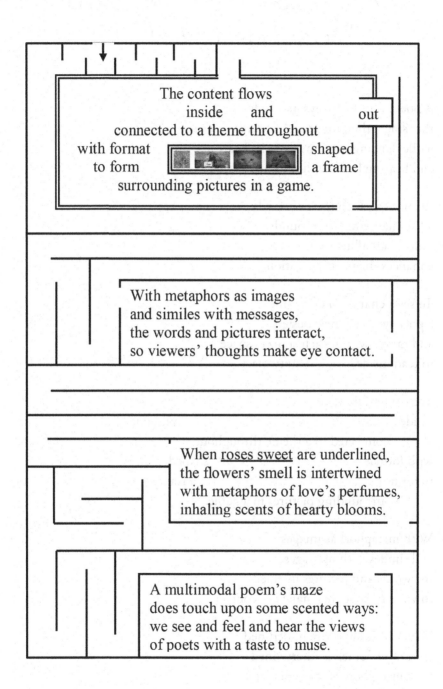

The content flows
inside      and           out
connected to a theme throughout
with format                    shaped
to form                        a frame
surrounding pictures in a game.

With metaphors as images
and similes with messages,
the words and pictures interact,
so viewers' thoughts make eye contact.

When roses sweet are underlined,
the flowers' smell is intertwined
with metaphors of love's perfumes,
inhaling scents of hearty blooms.

A multimodal poem's maze
does touch upon some scented ways:
we see and feel and hear the views
of poets with a taste to muse.

# Multimodal Poetry on World Poetry Day (March 21)

A poem's start conveys its words
that sing a rhyming song like birds
while dancing rhythms from its heart
and hearing beats within its art.

As musical discourse surrounds
all similar letters and sounds,
some aural alliteration
enhances the poem's creation.

To see a change in every line,
a poet eyes each new design
and moves within each stanza's space
to read inside _____ empty place.

The content flows
inside                                    and out
     connected to a theme throughout
with format                    shaped
to form                                    a frame
     surrounding pictures in a game.

With metaphors as images
and similes with messages,
the words and pictures interact,
so viewers' thoughts make eye contact.

When roses sweet are underlined,
the flowers' smell is intertwined
with metaphors of love's perfumes,
inhaling scents of hearty blooms.

A multimodal poem's maze
does touch upon some scented ways:
we see and feel and hear the views
of poets with a taste to muse.

# Easter (The First Sunday after the Paschal Full Moon)

The armoire's form was wooden, strong, and tall
while holding drawers with jewelry to enthrall;
two anxious hands did try to swiftly find
some earrings to wear with Easter in mind.

"My cross earrings aren't here, which really is weird.
Could they possibly have just disappeared,
like Jesus did years ago on Easter day
when He didn't with death in a tomb stay?"

"I've seen so many miracles in our world;
your golden earrings could have somewhere whirled,
but perhaps they're in a tough place to find
because you have so much jewelry entwined."

"I'm thankful for all of the things we own,
and I love wearing earrings so well known
as being symbols of Christ's sacrifice,
which saved us by paying for our sinful vice."

"Jesus Christ did pay for us a high price:
He allowed Himself to be a sacrifice,
so we can be sin-free in reality
and live great lives for all of eternity."

"Our Lord helps us in many positive ways
to live daily when every day's a maze.
As I look for my Easter earrings some more,
I pray He'll help me to finish this chore."

The anxious hands pulled out every drawer
while anxious eyes looked closely to explore
each space to try and find the earrings gold
inside a part of the jewelry's stronghold.

When checking in the highest drawer's largest space,
the anxious eyes paused to see a box in place
that had gone unnoticed while her search was wrong
because the empty box did there belong.

The box seemed larger than the earlier one
that she had placed inside the drawer for fun
to just contain nothing but empty space
in case new jewelry needed its own place.

Her eyes did stare at the box's large shape
while anxious hands removed the cover's tape,
which made the box's top open and rise,
revealing to all an Easter surprise.

Some Easter gifts were in the box's space
with designs that formed a Jesus showcase
of many items with a story to share
in logical order in the box's square.

"Thanks for this impressive surprise today;
it shows Christ's journey to Easter Sunday!
Instead of seeing that something is missing,
I'm glad to think of Jesus as living."

Two earrings were shaped like palm trees to shine
their branching green leaves, which now did align
beneath a necklace's picture of paws
of a donkey stepping on coats amid applause.

An image of Christ did the necklace transform
to a joyful Palm Sunday golden form

of Christ riding the donkey triumphantly
with crowds cheering His Jerusalem entry.

The next necklace showed the disciples all
eating their Last Supper with Christ sitting tall.
He compared their bread to his body divine
and connected His blood to drinking their wine.

"Then he took a loaf of bread, and when he had given thanks, he broke
it and gave it to them, saying, 'This is my body, which is given for you.
Do this in remembrance of me.' And he did the same with the cup after
supper, saying, 'This cup that is poured out for you is the new covenant in
my blood'" (Luke 22:19–20 NRSV).

Another necklace had a picture neat
of Jesus washing clean the dirty feet
of his disciples while he appeared to be
on both his knees before a table lordly.

"You call me Teacher and Lord—and you are right, for that is what I am.
So if I, your Lord and Teacher, have washed your feet, you also ought to
wash one another's feet" (John 13: 13–14 NRSV).

The next closest necklace showed Jesus in prayer
when an angel from heaven in midair
did visit, listen to, and strengthen him
to make more positive his moment dim.

More necklaces showed the arrest of Christ
and his journey before his sacrifice
upon a cross while wearing a thorny crown
to save many Christians from going down.

The missing earrings were sitting above
a similar necklace newly part of
the box's group of Easter jewelry,
which all did tell of Jesus's glory.

Less-anxious hands removed with loving care
the boxed-up jewelry to new places where
each item was glowing to now be free
within a larger drawer where there was more glee.

"I'll wear the earrings and necklace today
that show the resurrection of Christ to stay
with his disciples for forty more days
before his ascension to heavenly ways."

"I love your choice of jewelry for church today;
it's so nice to wear symbolic items on Easter Sunday.
All of the other jewelry is shining bright
and showing joy to have some added light."

"If I leave these drawers open all the time,
we'll have reflected light super sublime
to brighten many views every day and night
from jewelry unblocked for our sight's delight."

All jewelry brightly boxed to celebrate
Holy Week's joyful wonders could create
more love in the world and futures in heaven
if found to be free again and again.

Farley: A Happy Dog

# Gardening Secrets On National Gardening Day (April 14)

Though Arden and Clover did hide from view,
while wearing masks, they craved a garden new;
they opened their underground vault and eyed
a briefcase, photos, and more things inside.

While smiling, Clover said, "That's really great!
We still have room in here, so we'll not wait,
but rather we'll decide together how
to plant these plants that'll hide our vault right now."

Farley, their dog, walked over to the vault
and sniffed around before being forced to halt
by his owners, who both said, "Stay over there,"
while waving their hands like wind amid the air.

When Farley ran over to a big tree's trunk,
his giant fluffy paws appeared strong, but shrunk
by the shadow of the tree with its big roots
growing from the ground in amazing routes.

Arden pointed between the vault and tree;
"The perfect spot's here, where we'll walk darkly
among the plants and use the vault's doorway
to shelter our hidden secrets okay."

"Tomatoes will distract our neighbors all,
who'll be blinded by staring at food small.
This tree's big roots will stop the weeds and bugs;
the plants'll then need less water, food, and drugs."

When Arden heard the word "drugs," he snickered;
"do you really mean 'drugs' or a better word,
like 'chemicals' or some kind of 'playthings,'
like us tying plants to sticks with these strings?"

With a single laugh and a lengthy grin,
Clover used gardening tools to begin
to dig some tiny holes where plants could stay
attached to sticks and maybe live okay.

Arden brought Farley back into their house;
he then returned to help his working spouse
to decide how and where to place the plants
to keep them safe from fights with bugs like ants.

Tomato plants were taken out of pots
and quickly placed into the newest spots;
their stems were tightly tied to bamboo sticks
to brace the stems' support of thieving tricks.

These plants appeared to be planted so wrong:
their tiny roots were next to stones too strong
and were pressed against a tree's roots like trash
near the underground vault waiting for cash.

Too little space was left for enough soil
to nourish tiny roots to move and toil
within the grime of working just for life
to grow within a world of too-much strife.

With raging leaves, a small tomato plant
made lots of noise and scared a tiny ant,
which ran away as all new plants complained
to other plants about their stems too chained.

The noisy leaves appeared to be trying
to hit the vault, to escape from their string,

and to depart from the tree's roots so big;
no space was left, even for thieves to dig.

The tomato plants kept moving their leaves,
waving green with anger strong at both thieves;
the plants so wanted some light from the sun;
the thieves had shaded them, so they had none.

The thieves hid thirty-three thousand in cash
inside the vault before they made a dash
for their cabin's door and refused to hear
the sounds from their complaining plants so near.

The thieves, now indoors, spoke like thieving pros
and thought their words would only be shadows,
so plants, animals, and other people
would never hear their ideas deceitful.

"I'm so glad, Arden, about messing up
while holding my luggage and coffee cup
at the airport, not being too awake,
and grabbing the wrong briefcase by mistake."

"I'm fairly certain you grabbed the wrong case
on purpose and even did choose to place
our briefcase near that rich-looking stranger,
who noticed too late a switch did occur."

"You know I try to never lie to you,
so why would I be hiding something true?"
Clover removed her mask and dropped it down
upon the floor while her closed mouth did frown.

"Without that mask to hide your lying face,
your expressions do visibly erase
your claim to truth with a mouth that's frowning
and eyes that are staring down, still hiding."

Clover's angry eyes at Arden did glare;
Arden removed his mask, threw it to where
Clover's was resting on the wooden floor
with nothing else to hide near the locked door.

"We both do know what'll too quickly happen
if we report the cases switched, Arden.
We'll have to tell the police all about
that man's actions and political clout."

"That guy could have been carrying that cash
to do governmental tasks in a flash."

"Most people these days have to multi-task;
a brief case can be an office fast mask."

"A perfect brief case is a timely place
that connects our tasks to a moving space."

"I know that guy was committing a crime
to travel with so much cash this one time
and maybe other times, so reporting him
will only hurt us and make our lives grim."

"A politician with that much money
hidden in his briefcase was probably
planning to trade luggage at the airport
with that person who was tiny and short."

"Their interactions were interesting.
Before the politician saw something
about his briefcase that differed a bit,
the short person told him all about it."

"I'm glad you talked me into leaving then,
so we escaped the vision of those men

while walking really fast to hide your theft
and reaching that bus right before it left."

"We'll just have to be quiet about this,
so we can be safe with nothing amiss;
we don't want to be accused of doing
whatever those criminals were doing."

Arden sighed. "I'll try hard to not betray
your secret, so we can happily stay
inside our home, where we can safely dwell,
instead of living in a prison cell."

"Thanks so much for being understanding;
your support will help keep our vault standing,
so cash, heirlooms, papers, pictures, and keys
will be like tomatoes with no disease."

"Your garden idea's a creative thing,
so we can make believe we're gardening
while we're really just seizing some more cash
from the inside of our vault's secret stash."

While hiding dark in their masks every night,
the thieves did use a single flashing light
to sneak into their vault and grab money
without helping their plants under the tree.

For three more weeks within the tough setting,
the tomato plants did grow by twirling
their roots around the roots of the big tree
and moving close to the vault with no glee.

The plants couldn't use money in the vault
to buy plant food for their hunger to halt,
but they still did try to grow roots and leaves,
which helped to hide a vault for heartless thieves.

With sad and drooping leaves turning yellow,
the plants continued to work and to grow
by squeezing paths for all of their sickened roots
while thieves kept stepping on the roots with their boots.

The boots were too heavy for roots to fight;
the boots did injure a root every night
without the stupid thieves even knowing
the damage they were constantly doing.

While outside one night to open the vault,
Clover and Arden did not want to halt,
but stepped on many roots of tomatoes,
took some cash, moved their flashlights, and then froze.

The plants were fighting to loosen their ties
to bamboo sticks while trying hard to rise
and use their rage to hit and trip the thieves
with the horror of their yellowing leaves.

"The plants seem really mad at life tonight."

"It's maybe just too much wind and no light."

"They seem quite upset when the wind does blow;
maybe they're asking for our help to grow."

"We soon, Arden, can eat tomatoes ripe
and love the flavors of each different type
while the plants work hard and help us as thieves
by hiding our vault with their stems and leaves."

"Will water and food help the plants to grow?
Many leaves have changed from green to yellow."

"We're too busy to spend more time out here;
the plants know nothing and won't even care."

"We placed them under this tree's shading ring,
so everyone will think we're gardening."

"We should just look like we're in the garden
each time we go into our vaulted den."

"You keep rubbing your face. Are you thinking,
or without wisdom teeth, are you hurting?"

"The dentist gave me a root canal, too,
so now I'm partly like our plants that grew
their roots in canals, leading to disputes
that'll hurt themselves and maybe other roots."

"I think the plants want to dispute us, too,
because of their angry waves at me and you;
I'm glad we looked at all of them tonight
while wearing masks to stay hidden from sight."

"Plants know not about us and dental pain,
but even without some plant food and rain,
our tomatoes in a few weeks will be
a great food to eat for you and for me."

On a plant near the vault, some yellow leaves
now drooped in depression because the thieves,
hidden behind their masks, saw not the truth
about eating from plants with no wise tooth.

"Can we come here in daylight tomorrow,
so we can better see each tomato?"

"That sounds like a really great plan for us;
if we see problems, we can them discuss."

The next day, the thieves in sunny terrain
did see their vault, which the plants did disdain

by fluttering their sickened leaves away
from the steel door's demand for them to stay.

Clover was first to step too near the plants
while saying, "You guys are only transplants,
and you're acting like you really deplore
your job of hiding that vault and its door."

The tallest plant fell away from its stick
and moved a low branch that was slightly thick
in front of Clover's feet that were skipping
around while showing each untied shoestring.

Clover tripped, banged her hand on the vault's door,
and fell while screaming: "We're truly at war!"

The fallen plant waved sharpened leaves to chop
at Clover's hand to make her screaming stop.

She grabbed the plant's bamboo stick, broke it short,
used it as a helpful cane for support
while quickly standing up, and hit the plant,
making all of the leaves wave, gasp, and pant.

Arden yelled, "Why are you hitting that plant?"

"It attacked me and didn't stop its rant."

"That plant's been helping by hiding our cash."

"It still did trip me, like some kind of trash."

"The wind pushed that plant, making it trip you."

"The plant opposed not and with the wind flew."

"Since we're here before sunset in our boots,
you shouldn't be stepping on plants or roots."

"We came out in sunlight to better see
if these plants would stay alive and healthy,
so we'll eat their fruit while they hide our cash,
but they're treating us bad, like we're the trash."

On two of the leaves, some dampness did grow
and appeared to be tears of painful woe
emanating from leaves broken in full
with cuts in the leaves very visible.

"The plant you hit is crying now in pain;
without enough sunlight, plant food, or rain
to make tomatoes in a healthy way,
but it's still shrouding our vault's door okay."

"It's working for us while in our employ."

"It's growing food, too, for us to enjoy."

"Farley, our dog, so loves to eat our food,
and ripe tomatoes by dogs are safely chewed."

Several plants did wave their leaves sweetly
at the injured plant as it tried to be
with the others a working plant renewed
to hide the vault's money while growing food.

As Clover dropped the stick onto the ground,
she said, "Those plants are all turning around,
waving leaves at the hurt plant, and looking
too helpful. Plants can't do that kind of thing!"

"It's just the wind that's making the leaves wave,
but if winded plants helpfully behave

with just their plant stems and not a brain stem,
we should be more helpful to all of them."

As Clover looked at all the waving leaves,
her angry eyes shifted around like thieves
that wanted to steal some strength from the wind
as it hit her eyes while leaves of plants grinned.

Then Arden opened the vault's metal door
and said, "I want to now explore some more
of our treasures hidden beneath this tree,
instead of grabbing just bits of money."

"It'll take us some time, but I think you're right.
To look at everything with so much light
will help our eyes and minds to clearly see
if things are hidden, like fallen money."

As he and Clover together did stare,
some bills did fly within the windy air
and removed some dirt as their daily chore
by rubbing against the vault's metal door.

When Clover smiled at the dirtiest bill,
it flew upward above her head to spill
some dust into her mouth now open wide;
the smile did merge into a frown (to hide).

As Clover spit out the dust from the bill,
she growled in anger at the money's skill
to make her launder the dirt on its form
by using her spit to itself transform.

"Are you laundering that money, Clover?
It now looks damp, but it's not much cleaner."

"The money's now laundering its own self
while using my self, rather than its self."

Spitting lots more on the pile of money,
Clover then gazed at Arden's eyes in glee.

"While it looks like I've only spit some mud
onto bills while sounding each noisy thud,
I've partially cleaned our stash of money
by adding water to its scenery."

As Arden frowned, his eyes did jump around
within the vault's hidden heart underground
to see if all of the encased objects
were safe enough from dampening effects.

Under heavy mud, the money did pay
for its safety and did not blow away
into the real world without a safe case
to just enclose its self like a briefcase.

On a wall of the vault near the doorway
were more than ten keys hanging all okay,
hidden safe from the mud and windy things
while waiting to be used for openings.

"Those keys can unlock many homes and cars
of people who think of themselves as stars
that shine their light upon this crazy world
to help make our paths straight, instead of curled."

"My paths, Arden, are never very straight,
but yours are always so perfectly great
that I know your mazes are amazing,
whether they turn, go straight, or both ways swing."

"Thanks, Clover, but you're a strong supporter,
whose strength is tall even though you're shorter
than many other people in our lives;
you often greet others with your high fives."

"We have here many keys for the safety
of items and in case we lose a key."

"To look at these numerous keys is fun;
each often connects us to a loved one."

"I'm thinking about items in our stash.
Are any more important than the cash?"

"Yes, many are. For some of the photos,
we don't have other versions to transpose."

"My spitting should not these photos have hurt
'cause the photos beneath glass we did insert."

The photos in frames had glass protection,
so dampness had not hurt the collection
while the wind did clean some dust from the glass,
so viewers could see the pictures en masse.

Atop the stack of photos tall was one
of people having some gardening fun
while planting plants that they all did prefer,
weeding weeds, and watering with water.

All gardeners had help from wasps and bees,
as a photo captured these insects as keys
to unlocking protection from problems
related to bugs and no pollen on stems.

"Back then, I used to spit to water plants;
I hated gardening because of ants,

80

but now, I love these pictures of loved ones
and miss gardening with my family tons."

"These days, we have each other every day
and often visit our family okay;
since the vault is hidden by the plants near,
can we invite our family to come here?"

"The vault will be seen by most of the kids,
and even if they all close their eyelids,
they'll still view and want to open the door,
especially if it's locked up some more."

"That cash is stopping us from family fun;
we should be here with loved ones in the sun,
instead of hiding ourselves like we're locked
inside a vault with no keys to unlock."

"This photo of family fun is neat;
while I didn't like working in the heat,
I enjoyed that moment of honesty
when we were all truthful about that tree."

"You once did tell me about carving things
through the bark of a tree into its rings."

"I also told my parents all about
carving some words and pictures to shout out
my wishes for a better planting life
with more love, more smiles, less work, and less strife."

"Are the deep tree carvings in that photo
the plants that you carved and wanted to grow?"

"Yeah, they showed and still show my desires true
for positive items in life to view."

"I really love that picture of the tree
with carvings done by you so honestly
to ask for smiles and hearts with happiness
through shapes and words like 'play more' and 'stress less.'"

"My parents too did love my honesty
about carving in the bark of that tree;
they even loved my drawing of a heart
upon a living tree with smiling art."

"If you could now just study that photo,
you'd see more of your honest self and know
the strength of many smiles and hearts to love
one's truth and lack of lies when seen from above."

While Clover did stare at the photo's tree,
her expression showed her desire to be
more like her true self that had once been okay
and had lived in a more positive way.

"Like then, if I was now honest and wise,
I could stop hiding my true self with lies
and could then take off this mask that's too hot
for hard work, even in this shady spot."

"Are you thinking of talking to the cops,
or do you want to do more for our crops?"

"I'll think some more about our options best,
but we might be safer if I'm honest."

They both looked at their other hidden things
inside the vault until Arden said, "Rings."

Opening a box of hidden jewelry,
Clover's muddy hands used a dirty key

and removed rusty rings to be displayed
with no bright sun, but rather just some shade.

When Arden frowned at the rings not-golden,
Clover hid them back in their box again.

Then Arden did open a metal case
to check the papers inside and erase
any dust or dirt that did itself implant
atop all the documents most important.

"A streak of mud on top of number one
in this paperwork needs to be undone,
so my birth year changes from this seven
to make me six years younger once again."

"Did you lie to me about your birth year,
Arden, and now while I'm standing near,
you want to tell me the truth or deny
reality by adding to your lie?"

"You know that I'm always the truthful one,
who tells the entire truth to everyone."

She stared at Arden to see what he meant
before shaking her head in agreement.

Arden removed an old box from the vault
and placed it near a plant; the wind did halt.
He opened the box's top and then froze;
within the box were more books and photos.

"These all look great, but none of them are mine.
Are any connected to your family's line?"

Clover said, "Those books and photos for years
belonged to my grandparents, who had fears

that I would never become very good
because I sometimes lied and wore my hood."

"Did they ever read that bible to you?"

"They read it to lighten my darkened view."

"I know you were often depressed back then.
Was joy launched when the bible did open?"

Clover smiled. "I felt so safe and happy
whenever I heard a Godly guarantee;
the bible reading times were also great
for loved ones who'd travelled through heaven's gate."

"I didn't know that you believed in God;
you never told me; telling me now's odd."

"I never thought that you wanted to know;
plus my memory's making my honesty grow."

"You're actually even talking more
than what you normally have done before."

"To see our treasures through this open door
is making me want to be openly honest a whole lot more."

"When you were young and with your mom and dad,
did trips to church help you to feel less sad?"

"My parents and grandparents were always
too busy on Sundays and other days,
so we went to our church very rarely
but when we went, many truths did I see."

"Did you have a favorite bible verse
that helped your sadness to pause or disperse?"

The bible was opened by Clover's hands
as she said, "This one verse appears and stands
so often before me, and I wonder why
its meaning I've waited so long to apply."

The bible was opened to the right page,
so the verse to Clover's soul could engage:

"You shall not steal;
you shall not deal
falsely;
and you shall not lie
to one another" (Leviticus 19:11 NRSV).

"If you like this one bible verse, then why
do you often in your life steal and lie?"

"This verse sometimes appears to just me stun;
that doesn't mean it's my favorite one."

"What's your favorite verse, one that's helped you
to have a less-sad, more positive view?"

"For God so loved the world
that he gave his only Son,
so that everyone
who believes in him
may not perish
but may have eternal life" (John 3:16 NRSV).

"I've heard that verse so many times before.
Why do you and others that verse adore?"

"To think of giving makes me want to give
to those who need gifts for their lives to live."

"Even our plants need us to give them more
and to stop doing things to make them sore."

While watching more the wounded plant still strong,
Clover said, "You're right, and I've been so wrong;
if we help our plants more than we hurt them,
we'll feel like every tomato's a gem."

"With some plant food, water, and added light,
the plants'll feel more like working day and night:
they'll grow more tomatoes for us to eat
and will better hide our vault from the street."

"I'll give the plants some water and plant food,
and then I'll be in a much better mood."

"To help our plants will make me feel good, too.
I'll cut off tree branches, but just a few,
so this tree will be okay on its site,
and the plants will have a little sunlight."

While Clover and Arden finished their tasks,
they knew that they were still wearing their masks,
which is how they always did try to dress
whenever they wanted to be seen less.

When the garden tasks were all completed,
the broken plant was well watered and fed;
it raised its branches in a smiling form
and helped the thieves to even more transform.

Arden shifted his mask and asked unbarred:
"Why are we still hiding in our own yard?"

"If cops stop by, masked thieves will be at fault
for hiding money in our hidden vault."

"Because of personal items happy,
the cops will still blame us for the money."

"If we keep wearing our masks, in a flash,
we can blame strangers for hiding the cash."

"I hate to keep hiding myself outside.
I want honesty on my face with pride."

While removing her mask, Clover did say,
"The bible, love, and plants have shown a way;
I'll go to the cops with the hidden cash
from that brief case that I grabbed in a flash."

"That day, you grabbed the wrong brief case too fast;
when those people claim they're missing their stash,
the cops'll look at the airport's videos
and find us with help from license-plate pros."

The cops were soon told of the airport scene;
they said "thanks" to Clover for coming clean.
A politician, friend, and a crime ring
were arrested for money laundering.

Then Clover told Arden, "They said we're free,
won't be arrested, and can live safely
in our own home without a need to hide
from thieves and neighbors who near us reside."

"I'm glad we're free to live unhidden lives;
our self-esteem's implanted and survives."

"I no longer will steal a single thing;
I instead want to feel good by giving."

The gardeners no longer were hiding
in masks and darkness while now providing

water, food, and smiling words as implants
for themselves and many supportive plants.

Whenever they came outside as a team
with their licking dog helping them to seem
more loving and open with no hidden lies,
they looked very wise with their open eyes.

A month later, the plants were healthier
with totally green leaves that did prefer
to have people eat tomatoes to gain
the plants' strength to withstand a hurricane.

Tomatoes many hung on branches green
while circling the vault's entrance now clean
and shaped as a heart by the framing plants
that pierced the doorway's edges like implants.

"Our metal vault looks like a shining heart
with framing leaves and tomatoes to start
our next farming trip of treasures anew
for us to love with our hearts being true."

"Our plants are so much happier with help
from us and Farley, who often likes to yelp
his hunger by showing his happy tongue
and letting us see some helpfulness sprung."

To give to the world when seeing a lack
means thankfulness will pay the giver back
for loving, helpful routes in time and space
with treasures vaulted safely in a case.

An Adopting Cat

# An Adopting Cat On National Adopt a Shelter Pet Day (April 30)

After living with hunger her whole life,
the cat was rescued, but not without strife
from sirens, strangers, a cage in a van,
and a confusing, scary rescue plan.

With scratches on her legs, she tried to dash
away from bright, noisy lights that did flash
across her path 'til a blanket was thrown
atop her cries by a person unknown.

The cat named Cal was pushed inside a cage
and driven to a vet, who figured her age
while checking her health, scars, and scratches new
before giving Cal some food and shots, too.

Though Cal was too upset and scared to eat,
her visit with the vet was now complete,
so she was pushed into the cage again
and driven over potholes now and then.

After Cal did reach the rescue center,
into a larger cage, she did transfer,
but still she was scared and trying to hide
from strangers who saw her face as petrified.

Most people left to travel home that night,
and Cal did curl inside her blanket tight.
She was okay with all the other cats,
but she jumped from barking dogs and strangers' pats.

The morning's visitors had not yet appeared
when Cal did eat a bit while being scared.
Her eyes were jumping all around the room,
fearful of attack while food she did consume.

When people appeared near Cal to hear her purr,
she tried to hide in the furthest corner
of her cage's enclosing metal bars,
slightly hurting herself and adding to her scars.

After a few days of strangers choosing cats,
Cal knew the kittens were always getting pats;
she wanted to help the cats of her age
or older to escape from life in a cage.

Each night after people had left the room,
Cal would look at the food each cat did consume,
eat a little food, rub her cage's door,
and show her cat friends she did them adore.

Whenever another cat did stare at Cal,
she'd blink her eyes and look to a new locale,
which told the other cat that she was trying
to be humble, peaceful, kind, and loving.

When only cats were in spots in the room,
Cal would lick her fur-less scars and herself groom;
she'd walk in circles with her tail held high,
which displayed her happiness to have friends nearby.

A video camera showed the cat's room
to the center's employees in the backroom;
they all knew that Cal loved cats while being
too fearful of people, dogs, and bruising.

When six long months had passed with constant stress,
this gorgeous Calico cat was still homeless;

people kept choosing the younger, loving cats
that engaged in head-bumps to ask for pats.

A potential adopter then came in
and said that a cat-loving cat would win;
she needed a cat that would love her ill cat
and would befriend this cat with no combat.

When Cal tried to hide in her cage's corner,
the adopter still wanted to adopt her
because she knew how to help an anxious cat
and thought that Cal was a cat diplomat.

Some other gorgeous cats needed homes, too;
the adopter did donate to help a few
while choosing Cal for being there too long
and for being too thin and scared but strong.

When Cal was taken while crying with fear,
into her forever home's atmosphere,
she smelled two other cats who were living there
and calmed down a little when they came near.

The cage was opened where Cal could safely hide
in a room with a gated door to provide
a private spot for Cal to acclimate
herself within a forever home great.

After a week of staring and blinking eyes,
the other rescued cats did publicize
their adoption of one another as friends
by licking their friends through the gate's open ends.

While Cal was still too scared of her owner
to give purrs and rubs to this homeowner,
she soon was eating without being scared
of being attacked in the home she now shared.

The owner helped Cal and her fluffy fur
to have a loving, rather than a scared, purr
by using gradual actions with toys
and pats and hugs to add to the cat's joys.

The adoptee Cal became an adopter
when she helped the ill, depressed cat to purr
by rubbing his thinning fur, licking his face,
and keeping him warm by sleeping near his space.

After three months in a home with everything,
Cal was purring, licking, rubbing, and loving
the other cats, the adopter, and the food
by adopting them all with her loving mood.

# A Maze Poem: Amazing Roads on the National Day of Prayer (First Thursday of May)

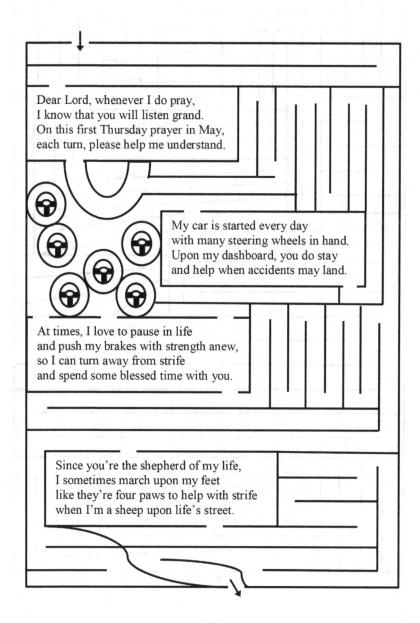

Dear Lord, whenever I do pray,
I know that you will listen grand.
On this first Thursday prayer in May,
each turn, please help me understand.

My car is started every day
with many steering wheels in hand.
Upon my dashboard, you do stay
and help when accidents may land.

At times, I love to pause in life
and push my brakes with strength anew,
so I can turn away from strife
and spend some blessed time with you.

Since you're the shepherd of my life,
I sometimes march upon my feet
like they're four paws to help with strife
when I'm a sheep upon life's street.

I love your blessings truly seen
to brighten lives on every day;
with lights of yellow, red, and green,
each journey is its own freeway.

With yellow lights, we often speed,
instead of going very slow.

With red for lights, a stop's decreed,
so we should stop, not pausing-go.

With green for lights, we mostly need
to just make sure our tires do go.

Your presence always I adore,
but still I drive and make mistakes;
instead of pausing for rapport,
I drive too fast without my brakes.

Then when I'm speeding even more,
I pause to see some evil snakes
that hit and break my auto's door,
before they bite and cause headaches.

I quickly step upon my brakes
and pray the snakes are on the floor
beneath the pedal for the brakes,
so snakes will break, just like the door.

Instead of stomping feet to keep
a fight ongoing with the snakes,
I should be helping them to leap
into your land of good remakes.

I'll push my inner horn to beep
at all of my unearthly quakes
while praying for your love to keep
me miles from sin and more mistakes.

Because of Jesus giving free
his life for sins of Christians true,
when prayer arrives to you from me,
forgiveness comes to me from you.

When sin has gone away from me
my thanks are sent to you, your son,
and Holy Spirit, loving three,
for all you've finished once begun.

With bible verses, many words
do speak your truth for me to hear;
at church, the songs of friendly birds
all sing their love for blessings near.

I'm learning more from rhythmic words
and hearing sermons made to steer
my driving close to God's great words
with lighted signals made to cheer.

I'm thankful, Lord, for all you do;
you help to keep my windshield clean,
so I can see your blessings true
when snow or rain falls on my screen.

To drive within my life is great,
for I am free to drive to you
on curving roads or ones so straight
they lead to registrations new.

I love my car's new license plate;
I vow to pray again again
and drive through gates that you create
to stay on roads to you. Amen.

# Amazing Roads on the National Day of Prayer (First Thursday of May)

Dear Lord, whenever I do pray,
I know that you will listen grand.
On this first Thursday prayer in May,
each turn, please help me understand.

My car is started every day
with many steering wheels in hand.
Upon my dashboard, you do stay
and help when accidents may land.

At times, I love to pause in life
and push my brakes with strength anew,
so I can turn away from strife
and spend some blessed time with you.

Since you're the shepherd of my life,
I sometimes march upon my feet
like they're four paws to help with strife
when I'm a sheep upon life's street.

I love your blessings truly seen
to brighten lives on every day;
with lights of yellow, red, and green,
each journey is its own freeway.

With yellow lights, we often speed,
instead of going very slow.

With green for lights, we mostly need
to just make sure our tires do go.

With red for lights, a stop's decreed,
so we should stop, not pausing-go.

Your presence always I adore,
but still I drive and make mistakes;
instead of pausing for rapport,
I drive too fast without my brakes.

Then when I'm speeding even more,
I pause to see some evil snakes
that hit and break my auto's door,
before they bite and cause headaches.

I quickly step upon my brakes
and pray the snakes are on the floor
beneath the pedal for the brakes,
so snakes will break, just like the door.

Instead of stomping feet to keep
a fight ongoing with the snakes,
I should be helping them to leap
into your land of good remakes.

I'll push my inner horn to beep
at all of my unearthly quakes
while praying for your love to keep
me miles from sin and more mistakes.

Because of Jesus giving free
His life for sins of Christians true,
when prayer arrives to you from me,
forgiveness comes to me from you.

When sin has gone away from me
my thanks are sent to you, your son,
and Holy Spirit, loving three,
for all you've finished once begun.

With bible verses, many words
do speak your truth for me to hear;
at church, the songs of friendly birds
all sing their love for blessings near.

I'm learning more from rhythmic words
and hearing sermons made to steer
my driving close to God's great words
with lighted signals made to cheer.

I'm thankful, Lord, for all you do;
you help to keep my windshield clean,
so I can see your blessings true
when snow or rain falls on my screen.

To drive within my life is great,
for I am free to drive to you
on curving roads or ones so straight
they lead to registrations new.

I love my car's new license plate;
I vow to pray again again
and drive through gates that you create
to stay on roads to you. Amen.

# A Butterfly on Mother's Day
## (Second Sunday in May)

When leaves were attached to a rose's stem,
the rose's smell flew freely through the air
as children gave their mom the rose with gems
attached in jewelry that each leaf did wear.

The mom showed her youngest child how to take care
by watching for thorns on the rose's stem.
The mom then felt motions in and near her hair,
so she turned sideways to look for mayhem.

A butterfly waved its wings a foot nearby
the mother's shifted eyes that tried to stare
at wings while looking, too, at her kids close by
and wanting light from the rose's gems to share.

The mother's hands and children's eyes flew high
while mom did place a necklace atop her hair
to circle the beauty of the butterfly
and be a shining crown for her to wear.

The crown did fence the butterfly's journey;
its wings moved through the maze of necklace parts
until the wings exited and were free
to wave cheerful good byes to others' hearts.

The necklace's gems reflected their light
to enhance the butterfly's new journey
with shining extensions for wings in flight
and paw-shaped reflections for eyes to see.

The butterfly stayed near the golden light
that spread around the room with shining rounds
from within the necklace's gems very bright;
the children all wanted some necklace crowns.

The mom put her gifts of necklaces with glee
atop their heads without the butterfly's strife;
the lighted crowns would help her children to see
the roses, thorns, and butterflies of life.

To teach, admire, give love, and always share
are what a mom does while looking to stare.

# A Prayer Poem with Memories for Memorial Day (The Last Monday in May)

Dear Lord,
We thank you for the chance to remember
and honor the acts of each service member
who surrendered a life to help us to grow
within our lives with more history to know.

We love our freedom, safety, and country;
we live so close to each animal and tree;
they all grow freely in our land and stand tall
with freedom of space and paws to climb each wall.

The World War II and other memorials
help us to make many more memories
about our country's amazing history,
which connects to lives like the roots of a tree.

We ask in the loving name of Jesus Christ
that he will bless those who were sacrificed
(each service animal, woman, and man),
so others could have a better lifespan.

Amen.

# Historic Gaspee Days Parade
## (A Saturday in June)

The painted stripes of red and white and blue
did shoot along the gray-cemented road
to strongly express our country's thank you
to those whose desire for freedom did explode.

On June 10th, 1772,
"America's First Blow for Freedom"[5] did flame;
when the Sons of Liberty and others, too,
hated the *HMS Gaspee* for taxing maim.

John Brown, Abraham Whipple, and others who
attacked and burned the *Gaspee* did oppose
the wrongful British actions that did accrue
to give American colonists many woes.

With the number of ships being only eight,
the burning of the *Gaspee* was a spark
for future Americans to celebrate
with events in Pawtuxet Village and Park.

Many people on a Saturday in June
were watching the Gaspee Days Parade start:
they heard the noises of volunteers in tune
with their costumes that were historically smart.

Parading cannons and guns shouted loud
as American patriotic music played
some sounds of freedom amidst the clapping crowd
that was honoring heroes through the parade.

The Clydesdale horses, distanced from all guns,
did blink their eyes at the clapping diverse
while marching as strong as soldiers pulling tons
upon noisy roads with a maze to traverse.

To escape the noise, some birds flew away,
and fearful squirrels ran to other spots,
as parade-watchers jumped to hear the way
we'd been freed from British taxes and gunshots.

Whenever we hear the fearful sounds of war,
our knowledge of each heroic sacrifice
is enhanced by celebrating freedom more
with historic marching and sounds: once, twice, thrice, . . .

A Timely Cat on Father's Day

# Tools for Clocks on Father's Day (Third Sunday of June)

The children all smiled as their father gazed
at their gifted tools within a cardboard box;
he then removed each metal tool and raised
it high upon a shelf near broken clocks.

He showed his children how to fix a clock
by using three of the tools that were his gifts;
his kids did think they knew how to fix a clock
and tried to fix two other ones in shifts.

The kids had questions about the process
of fixing clocks with their dad's gifted tools;
multiple times, he did show and express
how tools could fix a clock with a maze of rules.

The children fixed two clocks in the next hour.
The three broken clocks were then all repaired.
The kids and dad did each other empower
when moving hands on the clocks were compared.

The fixed clocks all kept moving at the same time,
so everyone knew the timing was right
for clicking into the future to chime
with each memory of today's delight.

The dad put the new tools away, said "congrats,"
gave his kids the clocks to put next to their beds,
and asked, "Is this box a present for our cats?"
Three kids all said "yes" by shaking their heads.

The cats chased the kids and their dad as they moved
the cardboard box along a timely pathway;
the cats ran into the box and approved
its placement in their room for rest and play.

One of the cats jumped onto a chair's top
while the other one jumped into the box;
they both were making memories to swap
amid loved ones spending time via clocks.

When memories are made with clocks as gifts,
the presents become a chance to share some shifts.

# Historic Lights of Independence Day (Fourth of July)

While waiting for the fireworks display to start,
the parents listened to their children be smart
as they discussed revolution's horrors
for America's historic explorers
who needed to become independent
to free themselves and each future descendent.

"America's colonists hated armies
that stole their space within their colonies
while collecting unfair taxes from all
and dropping charters to force their laws to fall."

"Back then, King George the Third was the British king;
he wanted Separatists to do each thing
according to his tyrannical spree.
They even kidnapped Americans at sea."

"Thomas Jefferson initially did craft
and others did help to edit his draft
of the Declaration of Independence,
which made them free from British dependence."

When fireworks began with some noises loud,
the family in the middle of the crowd
became quiet with their dog that stepped a paw back
because it was scared about an attack.

The parents brought their kids and dog back home
and talked about having the freedom to roam
with softer noises around their own yard
while still seeing fireworks with high regard.

The peacefulness of owning one's own space
results in stronger feet and paws in one place,
so people and pets can freely all move
forward on paths in mazes that all approve.

After quieter fireworks exploded bright,
the dog began to overcome his fright;
while the exploding noise was still fearful,
the dog barked, raising his eyes untearful,
and then marched on his paws strongly forward
before stopping fast and jumping upward.

More about declaring freedom was heard
by the parents who listened to every word
and loved the constitutional remarks
of their children while their dog spoke in barks.

On the Fourth of July, history's fire
sent lights of independence to inspire
many groups of parents, children, and pets
to walk through life with feet and paws as assets
within a maze of streaming stars of light
that freely flash their independence bright.

International Spy Museum, Washington, D.C.

Kylie: A Spying Dog

# Spying Eyes on National Dog Day (August 26)

The service dog, Kylie, was in deed a spy:
when close to many people, she acted shy
while visiting the Spy Museum's objects
and watching for secret criminal suspects.

The cone atop Kylie's head was meant to be
a way to hide her camera's spying spree,
so she could appear tiny and unhealthy
while being strong and trained to be stealthy.

The spying dog was pulling her owner's hand
attached high on the leash as they had planned;
people would think the tall owner was in charge,
but the tiny dog had spy tasks quite large.

The dog let her owner pause for a short time
to view an historic exhibit sublime
with Washington's "Spying that Launched a Nation"[6]
displayed through a statue and information.

A hooded visitor walked past them too fast
while everyone else was slow in contrast;
the dog followed this person who seemed too stressed
and too fast to be a truly normal guest.

The fast visitor suddenly stopped and stared
at one exhibit that he then compared
to a picture on his cell phone's shaded screen
while acting like a spy in a movie's scene.

The spying visitor then looked around
at others who were slow to come and surround
the same exhibit's many projections
with lights pointing in different directions.

When no one was standing close to detect
the visitor's moves, he removed an object
from the pocket of his dark hoodie's left side,
so he could use it while it no more would hide.

The now unhidden object was seen to be
a cigarette lighter as a flame did flee
from its small metallic form to move up
near the venting system's air-grille setup.

The flame was too big to be coming out of
a normal cigarette lighter with no love
for the many burnable items nearby
and the many people who'd run to not die.

Tiny Kylie moved superfast to discern
what the spying person was trying to burn.
She pulled her owner toward the burning light
and wanted to win any upcoming fight.

The visitor's lighter kept flaming away
as he stepped behind the exhibit's display,
pulled a cigarette out of his pocket's space,
and moved it toward his hoody-hidden face.

When the cigarette was lit between his jaws,
the visitor did feel Kylie's front paws
jumping upon his boots while barks jumped out
of Kylie's mouth as a spy's way to shout out.

The visitor moved the lighter still flaming
toward his cell phone's location while exclaiming,

"Get your crazy little dog away from me,
or I'll burn this burner phone before I flee!"

From the cigarette and lighter, smoke flew up
toward the ceiling's vent before they blew up
the burner phone within its protecting case,
resulting in Kylie's owner using mace.

The visitor's eyes did water and blink
after feeling the lipstick's stream of mace ink
while Kylie's safety cone had quickly closed
to make her fighting face be not exposed.

The cloth hoodie was not enough protection
to keep the visitor safe from detection;
security officers stepped over fast
and a circle of safety quickly amassed.

The visitor dropped the lighter and phone
because his heated hands wanted to disown
the illegal objects well known to be hot,
but he still kept on smoking medical pot.

The lighter's flame stopped before hitting the floor,
but the phone's fire started flaming even more
with its quick fall right next to Kylie's spot;
she saw it and barked, but the flame didn't stop.

A small and clear window in Kylie's cone
protected her face and let her see the phone,
so she hit the burning phone with her cone's top,
causing the flame to immediately stop.

As a security person stared at Kylie,
her owner said, "A spy she's been trained to be;
at times, she uses her cone as a weapon,
and she sometimes lets it be her protection."

Karen Petit

"Our dogs do so much to help their owners;
without them, many of us would be loners."

The hooded visitor was smoking his pot;
he, Kylie, and others were coughing a lot.

An officer said with a coughing frown:
"Stop that smoking! You're spreading your smoke around."

"I have my medical pot paperwork!
When I'm sick, without smoking, I'd be berserk!"

"It's really against the law to smoke in here!
We've all been coughing. Are you able to hear?"

"The problem's that burner phone that I just found.
I burned it up, but it fell down to the ground."

"You're not supposed to burn up burner phones!
You should have given to us any lost phones!"

"Oops! I really didn't know I'd done a crime."
I'll try to do the correct thing next time."

Discarding half of his cigarette, while sad,
the visitor made everyone else glad.
No more smoke appeared anywhere to assault
their lungs; they thought the smoke was the smoker's fault.

The visitor pulled back his hood as he said,
"I'm sorry for all that smoke from just one med.
You helped me to know that my life needs to change,
so others won't be hurt when I need to use too many meds strange."

When the ex-smoker just went walking away,
the officers didn't force him to stay,

but instead thought that his honest posture's form
showed his goal to try to make himself reform.

Kylie pulled her owner to follow some more
the ex-smoker, who was exiting a door
to leave the museum, perhaps for a bus;
the owner was pulled by Kylie without fuss.

Once Kylie and her owner had looked around,
the ex-smoker was nowhere to be found,
so they didn't know if his change was real
or if he was doing a spy deal or steal.

When they arrived home, Kylie wagged her tail fast,
eyed her owner like a spy, and then asked
with her body language if she could see
videos from her camera's history.

They watched spy history with spying eyes
while sharing love with no reason to disguise
their presence, actions, views, and freedom found
without a leash to tie them down to the ground.

# Working for Honey on Labor Day
## (First Monday in September)

Like many so busy on Labor Day,
some bees were working without any pay;
while they had jobs to make honey for food,
their hive was crowded, small, and very crude.

To protect themselves, their jobs, and their hive,
the bees all worked together to survive
another day of trying to perform
their dances, climbings, and flights in a swarm.

The cleaners, foragers, and soldier bees
as members of different unions did seize
each chance to gain more pollen, nectar, and space
while protecting their boss in her queen-bee place.

The queen had extra space to work a lot,
but she wasn't in the uppermost spot;
her cells were at the bottom, far below
the pollen and honey, as all did know.

Some workers fed and groomed her every day
while others left the hive to stay away
until they had gathered their essential needs
from flowers, gardens, farms, a zoo, and weeds.

One bee, a cleaner, worked in the hive each day
until she was promoted on Labor Day
to become a forager finding some food
to eat and bring back to the hive's multitude.

She followed other workers outside the hive
to learn the paths they flew to safely survive
the outside world's attempts to them defeat
by stopping their lengthy search for nectar and pollen to eat.

The new and experienced foragers flew
to a group of plants in a nearby zoo,
where the animals were working hard to deal
with zoo visitors who made them anxious feel.

A bear near a tree in a fenced-in space
did growl at the bees in a nearby place,
making the bees emit their pheromones
to warn each other to leave for other zones.

The bees did leave the zoo and fly to a farm
to find more food from plants without doing harm;
the farmer did know that bees would help his plants
by pollinating and doing more than ants.

Inside the farm, some horses worked hard with guides
to carry people and backpacks for rides;
they walked past many chickens laying eggs
and cows producing milk to strengthen legs.

The bees next flew to a police station's yard
and passed over K-9 dogs standing guard;
near boxes and cars, officers were talking
while searching in the boxes and note-taking.

The dogs and police all looked very tired
after crime that last night had transpired:
the boxes had drugs from a dealer's offense
with lots of heavy crime-scene evidence.

The boxes were picked up and slowly carried
inside the station with sounds that were varied

for diverse jobs done by officers and dogs
while all were united to act like watchdogs.

One of them asked, "Can bees harm our sunflowers?
Too many of them have been there for hours
and seem to be eating the flowers and leaves;
I think they're all acting too much like thieves."

Voice two said, "Those bees really aren't stealing;
the nectar and pollen that they're eating
could perhaps be claimed by some to be stolen,
but bees help plants by moving the pollen."

Voice Three said, "Those bees are helping flowers;
while bees don't work non-stop for sixteen hours,
like we've done, they're still working very hard
to keep some food growing in every yard."

Four: "Even weeds that honey bees pollinate
can feed insects and cattle to keep them straight
in the middle of the amazing food chain;
the bees are helping all their food to maintain."

Five: "All animals, too, are working today,
and they're not getting any normal pay;
their paychecks are quite different from ours
but include extra food for extra hours."

The pollen baskets of the bees now were filled,
so the bees did ignore human words unskilled
at speaking to bees and different insects
even when some were criminal suspects.

The bees began their flight back to their hive
together in a swarm that did talk to strive
to keep each other as safe as they could
with pheromone smells about things no good.

With nectar and pollen both collected,
the bees were all flying unprotected
until they swarmed close to their hive and saw
some soldier bees stinging an animal's claw.

In front of their hive was a giant bear
that was hitting cells and trying to tear
all apart to find some of the bees' honey
on Labor Day without paying money.

The soldier bees kept on stinging the bear;
each bee did suffer a loss-of-life fear
of losing its own life when its stinger
would enter the bear and then there would linger.

The bear soon left with honey still in the hive
when twenty bees were no longer alive
while protecting themselves, their queen, and their food
from other lives that wildly did intrude.

The living bees swarmed together while trying
to do more tasks, so they'd be complying
with all of their boss's requested needs
to make more food with many added deeds.

By chewing some honey, pollen, and wax,
the bees made their storage cells from beeswax,
so honey, pollen, and the eggs of their queen
would stay safe when other animals were mean.

The newly promoted bee was helping lots
by waving her wings to clear moisture from spots
of nectar being changed to honey accrued
and sealed in the hive to be their winter food.

The cells created by so many bees
did fit together perfectly with ease

because of their waxed hexagonal forms
with sides all connected, even in storms.

The bees were a part of a living network
with workers and bosses united to work
in swarming hives while eating their honey
and together building their honey money.

# Sweetness on National Chocolate Day (October 28)

Atop a stove did stand a copper pan
enclosing cocoa, sugar, milk, and salt
with hugs of growing warmth that soon began
to override the top of chocolate's vault.

A spoon was flying fast with fudge's rise
and like a pet did squeak a message sweet
inside the pot's too tiny metal size
with heartless strength impaled by warming heat.

Across the pan's top edge, the candy flowed
and glided down the metal's outer sides;
the fudge's growing sweetness overrode
the hardness of a pan's now-hidden sides.

When sweetness shares itself, life's hardest trials
are hidden as chocolate in loving smiles.

D.C. Cat

Smithsonian National Museum of Natural History

Smithsonian Institution Building (The Castle), Washington, D.C.

National Archives Museum, Washington, D.C.

# Political Scratches from D.C.'s Dreaming Cat on National Cat Day (October 29)

In Washington D.C.'s National Mall
were people and animals near buildings tall.
All loved their freedom to dream of living life
in a democracy with lessened strife.

The homeless Cat was old enough to know
to sleep against a building's wall aglow
with warming air to help it stay alive
and dream of less stress and how to survive.

D.C. Cat's dream began on a round table
that was wooden without being too stable.
Atop other tables stood people and cats;
their noses shifted round while sniffing for rats.

The many humans and cats all jumped around
among each other's tables to switch their ground
until the room became a setting outside;
some jumped between cement and grass to collide.

Many people who were dressed very neat
walked too near the Cat and kicked their booted feet
to smash the puddled ground's water and scare
the Cat caged up in its feline nightmare.

The Dreaming Cat jumped up and ran too fast
in front of reporters doing a newscast;
the Cat scratched a statue to keep its claws strong;
a reporter yelled, "That cat's scratches are wrong!"

A politician talked to the reporter
and appeared to be a cat supporter,
but the anxious Dreaming Cat thought they were both
negative people hindering freedom's growth.

The politician touched two of the Cat's paws,
shook them like they were hands, and talked about laws
regarding the service of animals strong
to not work like criminals doing deeds wrong.

The Cat's claws extended themselves way too long
without wanting to slightly get along,
but rather wanting to scratch the human hand
that seemed to be claiming some space too grand.

A service animal's vest began to move
upon the hand still trying to improve
the Cat's understanding of its need to work
to help more people with some purring teamwork.

The frightened Cat couldn't calm itself down,
so when it heard angry words and saw a frown,
it thought the vest would cage its heart in jail.
The Cat flattened its ears while it thrashed its tail.

The suited human moved a large briefcase
near the angered Cat that hissed to keep its place
next to the museum building's warmest wall
and between two bushes not very tall.

Because the Cat from birth was feral always,
people made its life too much of a maze.
Whenever a container was placed too near,
the Cat disliked the loss of freedom idea.

When other cats came close and wanted spots
the same as the D.C. Cat's favorite spots,

they would negotiate with one another
while blinking eyes to accept each other.

When cats got together on a round table,
whether supporting links were weak or stable,
they would interact often with other cats
that were republicans or democrats.

The D.C. Cat wanted the freedom to roam
while owning its own round table and home;
its life would be better if it had more food
when making demands in an angry mood.

Political humans would often not see
the politics of cats as being a key
to unlock freedom's wealth to all for free
and helping all to defeat poverty.

A human contact, just a week ago,
had grabbed a friend of the D.C. Cat to throw
its scared self into a cat carrier's space
and bring its reality to some other place.

The D.C. Cat still remembered that act
and was dreaming partly about this contact
when the same human pushed the briefcase
in an angry way toward the hissing Cat's face.

The person pulled paper cash from the briefcase
while spitting more words into D.C. Cat's face
and pushing Cat's shoulders and fighting paws
into the case, which was scratched by Cat's claws.

The Cat kept pressing its lengthy, sharp claws
into the case's form without a pause
and tore open the leather, which made cash fly
to all people who were standing nearby.

"Vaccines" by the real human had once been said,
but the D.C. Cat heard hissing "scenes" instead;
the human's hand shoved into the briefcase
a syringed needle that neared the Cat's space.

The Cat escaped the case and clawed up the side
of a Smithsonian museum to hide
its dirty paws that often looked in trash
in order to find a needed Cat-food cache.

The politician, holding more cash, appeared
near the Cat on the roof where they both stared
at each other's shadowy, dirty forms
in the dream of the Cat that wanted reforms.

The staring eyes became political stairs
with steps of blinking eyelids from both pairs
moving one above the other in self pride;
the person stepped close to the Cat to collide.

The Cat attacked the giant stack of cash
because it thought the cash was illegal trash
that people moved while too close to each other
to take space away from one another.

The Cat's paws suddenly loved the money's feel;
it was much softer than the cement and steel
of the museums and statues nearby,
which could be seen from the roof high in the sky.

While scratching the pictured faces on the bills,
the Cat was giving to itself some thrills
because it thought its scratches made extra cash,
so people would love the added paper stash.

The human stepped next to the bills to be near
the cheer that changed the Cat's ugly nightmare

into happy dreaming with bills stacked for all,
so everyone could have a part of the haul.

The human wanted most of the pile of cash
and kicked the stack to make it fly and crash
into the top of the briefcase standing tall
while the cat's form transformed from large to small.

The syringed needle with liquid vaccine
moved and hit the cat, which thought it was mean
for humans to harm cats and steal their cash
when a Cat had just worked to create more cash.

The human then tried to scoop up all of the cash;
the Cat wanted its share of the paper stash,
so it could create with the bills a soft bed
like an outdoor nest with some warmth widespread.

The Cat and the human both touched the same bill;
with Washington's face turned toward Capitol Hill,
the image in money was moving so real
the D.C. Cat played with its toy-like appeal.

The Cat's group of claws on one of its paws
extended out to make the bill's motion pause
and distribute purrs from its paper form
to the claws and fingers trying to transform.

The Cat's vision connected the human's face
to the picture in the bill's central space;
within its dreaming world of playing a game,
both facial identities did look the same.

The D.C. Cat's eyes kept shifting up and down
between Washington's smile and the human's frown
when the human did tumble into a fall
while Washington's image was flying tall.

The fallen human's face now turned around
and stared at the dollar bill's pyramid crowned
with the Eye of Providence watching all,
so fallen people could again become tall.

The politician's hand touched the Cat's paws;
each touch became softer when thinking of laws
made by presidents and cats cashing in
on working together for freedom's win.

The cash was all divided between them both;
spreading cash would improve economic growth,
for more people and cats would spend their cash
on helping others with diplomacy's cache.

The D.C. Cat was still within its dream
when it jumped and landed in a spot supreme
in front of a house that was built for cats
with open doors and food for all diplomats.

The Dreaming Cat ran through an unlocked pet door,
rubbed its paws on a rug-covered wooden floor,
and jumped atop a couch's comforting form.
Freedom from hissing was now the Cat's norm.

It kept on dreaming of owning many spots
to help homeless people and animals lots
while jumping atop buildings with its paws
and purring creatively to help with the laws.

A Real Cat on Halloween

A Real Bird on Halloween

# Acting Like Pets on Halloween (October 31)

The children each looked like a different pet
in their costumes at the door of a vet,
who was giving away some treats to all
and being helpful while the rain did fall.

The child who was dressed like a puppy did say,
"I'll bark and bark on Halloween today
until I have another chocolate treat
to make my life a lot sweeter when I eat!"

The vet opened up his front door really wide
while picking up some pet food as he replied,
"Chocolate shouldn't be fed to a real dog,
and you're barking at me with your dialogue."

The child whose costume had cat pictures did say,
"He's barking like that just to act like a stray.
He's trying with his costume to entertain.
He also hates to walk around in this rain."

The vet talked as he waved the pet food and smiled:
"The youngest are the cutest, but the most wild.
Stray animals really need water and food;
in bad weather, like now, they may act too rude."

While meowing, the cat child rubbed her head
against the food in the vet's hands as she said,
"We'd love to help rescued animals to eat
and to help any strays we see on a street."

A third child chirped: "If you don't need that food for pets,
many animal shelters need such assets.
We can bring it all to help out a good cause
by walking there in rain with boots on our paws."

The children raised their feet to show off each boot
with pictures of pets to help them commute
through the mazes of life when each turn's a pause
that makes them wave hands with gloves shaped like paws.

The chocolate-loving "dog" raised a hand
to show his love for dogs and changed his demand:
"Rather than chocolate, can I have instead
that food, so sheltered animals can be fed?"

The other children all moved their handy paws,
clapping together in united applause,
while barking like dogs, chirping like singing birds,
and meowing like cats to speak their words.

The vet made animal sounds to show his love
for pets while using each hand as a glove
that moved like a paw while putting some cans
of food for animals into each child's hands.

The dog child's smile could be seen inside his mask
as he hugged the pet food and didn't even ask
for any chocolate for himself to eat
or for any other Halloween treat.

As the pet children started to step away
from the vet's house onto a new pathway,
the vet called them back and gave them more treats
of chocolate to add to their lives more sweets.

The purring cats, tweeting birds, and woofing dogs,
with squealing jumps from hamsters, rabbits, and frogs

put the food in their bags and clapped their hand paws
to show their happiness with much applause.

The rain stopped falling, so all was perfect
with puddles already made to reflect
the beauty of many hand and foot paws
of costumed children helping a petted cause.

The changed weather sweetened the upcoming maze
of walking on booted paws in different ways
to go to some animal shelters diverse
and leave pet food for centers to disperse.

The pairs of hands wearing paw-shaped gloves did wave
all together at the vet and to him gave
a happy night of seeing connections
between children and pets through paw reflections.

Sergeant Stubby in an Exhibit at the Smithsonian National
Museum of American History, Washington, D.C.

Smithsonian National Museum of American History, Washington, D.C.

# Rainbows on Veterans Day (November 11)

The D.C. monuments for veterans strong
were loved by tourists who were walking along
and remembering the actions of those
who had fought through rain to help us see rainbows.

Sergeant Stubby, a dog, won medals galore
for his help in battles of the First World War;
his biting attack of an enemy spy
ended in his promotion for his war cry.

Stubby very often did a dog salute:
when he saw soldiers do a human salute,
he would quickly raise his right paw up high
to position it above his right eye.

Courageous actions are done time and again
by veteran animals, women, and men;
many receive medals, like Simon the cat,
horses, pigeons, and dogs helping in combat.

The monuments and statues remind us all
of the courageous actions that did not stall,
but instead marched forth in a climate of war
on paws and feet to serve our country's core.

When storming noise brings thunder, snow, and rain,
military animals all act humane,
and service humans all act animated,
so our tears of rain will be sun-gated.

# A Thankful Prayer on Thanksgiving (Fourth Thursday of November)

Dear Lord,
I'm thankful, Lord, for your help in my life.
Especially when I'm encountering strife
and praying for your helpful, loving care,
many miracles do happen every year.

These miracles happen in the ways you think
are best to make my problems shrink,
so my blessed life improves even more
with each solution you bring to my door.

Doing my shopping last night was not a chore.
I found long lines at the grocery store,
but was really thankful to see lots of food
being bought by people in multitude.

When loving my family while we're meeting
on Thanksgiving Day for fun while eating,
we all are happy to have relaxing time
to spend with each other, which is sublime.

Our dogs are yelping now for more good food,
and our cats are all in a turkey mood;
we're thankful to spend some additional time
with loving pets that into our laps do climb.

We love the bible's words that help us each day
to connect to you every time when we pray;
we try to understand your suggested ways
to enhance our journeys with peace always.

"Do not worry about anything, but in everything by prayer and supplication with thanksgiving let your requests be made known to God. And the peace of God, which surpasses all understanding, will guard your hearts and your minds in Christ Jesus" (Phil. 4:6-7 NRSV).

Thank you, Lord, for giving each of us a life,
for forgiving us for errors in strife,
for giving us so much inside our lives,
and for uplifting us forever when eternity arrives.

In Jesus's name, we pray
to you today and each day,
Amen.

A Pet on Christmas Eve

# Gifted Pets on Christmas Eve (December 24)

On Christmas Eve, as people were sleeping,
three cats were awake and wildly playing
with one another in the Christmas tree
to find the best ornaments cat-friendly.

The cats were climbing 'round their tree's playground;
the branches kept on moving up and down,
so the attached ornaments were waving
to lure the cats into even more playing.

The ornaments with family photos
were rubbed with sweetness by every cat's nose
while ornaments shaped like balls and other toys
were scratched and batted into making noise.

Because of branches moving up and down,
a dog beneath the tree acted like a clown
with tilting head, flying paws, waving tail,
and barks that tried to tell a funny tale:

"The cats did open that present for cheer
this Christmas Eve, and claimed that I did tear
the paper off because I couldn't wait
any longer to see a wonder great."

A cat responded with meows to say:
"I cannot even see that well today.
How can you blame me for something you've done
while we're trying to have some Christmas fun?"

When people awoke and saw a paw-shaped rift
that looked most like the dog had opened the gift,
they laughed because the gift was for their cats
to wear on Christmas as their holiday hats.

A bit of paper sitting on the dog's head
did look like the wrapping paper green and red
still partially around the holiday hats
for the enjoyment of the playful cats.

The cats came out of the branches of the tree
while the dog was smelling the hats to see
if he should bite one to make it appear
like the paper on his head and fluffy hair.

One cat ripped open a different gift
that bounced and rolled out from its paper swift
while squeaking noise about its joy to be free
from its paper cage on Christmas Eve early.

One of the people laughed at the cat and said,
"Maybe that cat wanted us out of bed,
so he opened both of the presents with noise
and hoped that we would play with him and his toys."

The second person said, "The dog and that cat
were probably each trying to find a hat
for each other and help one another play
with some anticipation for Christmas day."

"It's nice they were opening just pet presents;
they're smart enough to know all the contents
inside the red and green wrapping paper
because they helped wrap things and smelled each vapor."

The second person laughed at pets' tails curly.
"They wanted to play with some toys early.

The cats helped by chasing each ribbon's trail
while the dog kept jumping and waving its tail."

"A part of Advent's pleasure is the way
we wait on Christmas Eve for Christmas day.
The birth of Christ is then looked forward to,
so we can all enjoy a Christmas new."

"Our pets don't know very much about dates,
but they sometimes have patience for what awaits
because we've trained them not to eat too early,
and they've only opened two presents early."

The pets ran in a gifted maze very swift
without unwrapping any other gift
while curious about each gifted action
that would result in more love and attraction.

The family and pets were animated
like others who, for many years, had waited
for the Christmas birth, then life and sacrifice,
of our loving Lord and Savior Jesus Christ.

Two Cats with Christmas Love

United States Botanic Garden, Washington, D.C.

United States Library of Congress, Washington, D.C.

# Scenes of Love on Christmas Day (December 25)

The Christmas stockings filled were tied together
with red and green bright ribbons to tether
their connections to one another strong;
the gifts would be seen while singing a song.

The music started when the children did sing
*Joy to the World,* as their parents did bring
a line of stockings all connected still
to each other and to a window sill
that displayed a nativity scene bright
with rays from the sky reflecting its light.

The brightly lit Mary, Joseph, and sheep
all looked toward the Infant Jesus, who was deep
within the manger's straw and reaching out
to touch a verse displayed in the scene's layout:

> "God's love was revealed among us in this way:
> God sent his only Son into the world
> so that we might live through him" (1 John 4:9 NRSV).

Light from the window-sill nativity scene
flashed along the ribbons all red and green
to land on stockings and begin the fun
of children who would look inside each one.

The children opened their stockings in shifts
and adored each other's similar gifts
while stockings were still connected to the sill
with the manger scene that was brighter still.

After the children had liked all their presents
of candy, socks, gift cards, tree ornaments,
CD's, jewelry, make-up, toothpaste, and cars;
the parents moved stockings near the cats' paws,
jiggled ribbons, shook each stocking side to side,
and encouraged the cats to look inside.

Both of the cats had fun pushing their paws
into the stockings to find treats for their jaws,
some catnip, toys for scratching, and noisy balls.
They next ran after lights shining on floors and walls
from laser pointers the children were moving
to excite some exercise for health improving.

The parents traded stockings with each other
and displayed their gifts one after another:
watches, pens, Christmas ornaments for their trees,
and manger scenes with camels, sheep, and donkeys.

One scene had shepherds near the manger merry,
with seven sheep, a donkey, Joseph, Mary,
and a flying angel smiling from above,
all looking at the infant Jesus with love
while a bible verse on the manger's form
was read out loud in a voice very warm:

> "The shepherds returned,
> glorifying and praising God
> for all they had heard and seen,
> as it had been told them" (Luke 2: 20 NRSV).

Wise men with gifts were in the second new scene
and displaying their gifts, so they could be seen
by Jesus as he lay in his manger's straw
close to an uplifted green and red paw
belonging to a camel who tried to reach
out with his paw in amazing body speech

to Mary and Joseph, who were standing near
a bible verse reference to Wise Men's cheer:

> "On entering the house,
> they saw the child with Mary his mother;
> and they knelt down and paid him homage.
> Then, opening their treasure chests,
> they offered him gifts of gold, frankincense, and myrrh"
> (Matt. 2: 11 NRSV).

Both manger scenes were placed on window sills new
and enhanced the living room's Christmas view
with bright reflections, so all of the pets,
children, and parents had merry mindsets.

The new ornaments were placed on the tree,
so their recent trip to the mall in D.C.
could be remembered by the people who went
and by the pets that each received a present.

Hands and paws touched the ornaments that were found
in D.C.'s stores and museums around
the Botanic Garden's scents and décor
and in the Library of Congress's store.

Their Washington trip was a blessing for all
as they helped each other to now install
their ornaments as memories of lives
to be stored as parts of future archives.

The feet, hands, and paws within the living room
all helped the Christmas tree to brighter bloom
by joining it to the manger scenes with prayers,
ribbons, stockings, and new ornament shares.

# Gifts of Pets on Birthdays

One twin wanted dogs for his birthday gift;
the other twin asked for cats as her gift.
The parents rescued both a dog and a cat
to live with love in their family's habitat.

The cat and dog knew each other already;
their shelter's training had made them ready
to get along encaged near other breeds
as long as they avoided aggressive deeds.

As the pets were carried into their new home,
they wanted to exit their cages and roam
within the setting with fewer sounds and smells
suggesting freedom from rescue-center cells.

When both of the pets heard children's applause,
they began to press their super-skinny paws
against their pet carriers' metallic doors
and tried to escape from the noise on all fours.

The twins ran over to the carriers
to open up the doors that were barriers
enclosing both of the pets that now were scared
of the noisy actions of two kids who cared.

Before the doors were opened, a voice said, "No!
We need to wait until these pets can show
that they've been trained to like one another,
so they will not attack and hurt each other."

The twin that most wanted two dogs did say,
"I think this great dog can be trained okay,

but I've heard that cats are much tougher to train
because they're often scared of losing terrain."

While shaking her birthday hat atop her head
to show her agreement, the cat-loving twin said,
"The cat and the dog look so scared right now;
we should hug them both and calm them down somehow."

One of the parents smiled while softly saying,
"We could help the most with food and game-playing,
and wait on hugs 'til they know us and our home
while being free in different rooms to roam."

The other parent wanted to try and test
the new pets to see if they were more stressed
when moved very close to each other's place
while still within each cage's separate space.

The cages were moved with the doors still closed,
but the cages were close together posed;
the two closed doors were touching each other,
so the new pets could reach out to each other.

The dog licked his door and extended his tongue
through an opening between two bars that hung
from the framing plastic container's form
that could train new pets if they needed reform.

The cat did stare at the happy dog's face
before stepping close into his breathing space,
smelling, and then licking his tongue with her own,
which showed they were to each other well known.

"They must have been friends in the rescue center,"
said a parent as more joy did enter
the faces of pets together displaying
their love for each other and hopes of staying.

The twins slid both of the cages apart
and wanted their new pets' freedom to start;
the metallic doors were quickly opened wide,
but the cat tried to move backwards to hide.

The dog-loving twin laughed twice while he asked,
"Why has our new dog ran out to us so fast,
while the cat's in the cage's corner to hide
from the doorway leading to freedom outside?"

"She's acting just like many scared cats do
whenever they smell, hear, or see settings new,"
said the other twin. "She likes the other pet,
but might be worried about seeing a vet."

"You could be right," one of the parents said.
"While our house smells like two pets, not a hundred,
most rescue-center animals must go
to see a vet, get shots, and have more woe."

The cat's cage was moved to a smaller room;
some food was left nearby to cheer up her gloom.
Once she was alone, she exited her cage
to eat the food she'd love until an old age.

When the parents and twins together did sing
"Happy Birthday" while standing in a ring
around the kitchen table's birthday food,
the dog's happy tail and barks conveyed his mood.

The cat became curious, snuck close, and looked
into the kitchen's space to see what was cooked
for the birthday dinner's meal that smelled so great
and was in the same room as her new playmate.

The fish smelled perfect; other smells did not.
The cat moved slowly while scared of being caught.

The people all watched without scaring her more,
so she wouldn't run out of the kitchen's door.

The twins gave to both the dog and the cat
some fish in bowls next to where their paws were at;
the cat looked around, saw the dog eating fish,
and then began to eat her own from her dish.

The dog was the first to eat all of his fish;
he sauntered over too close to the cat's dish.
She stared for three seconds at his staring eyes,
cried a tiny cry, and pushed her paw to rise.

The dog then knew she needed lots of food,
just like many of the animals rescued
from settings that lacked the essentials of life
and included many instances of strife.

As the dog stepped away from the cat's bowl,
the dog-loving twin moved toward the dog's bowl
and placed many pieces of fish fillet
to fill up the empty dish all the way.

While seeing his act, the cat-loving twin said,
"I know you love fish to be between your bread,
but it's so neat that you're giving him food
on our birthday to show him your gratitude."

The dog wagged his tail when he saw more fish;
his paws moved fast to bring him near his dish.
While the people all shared their birthday food,
they talked about their pets' in a birthday mood.

New pets are gifts of additional kin,
loving each other as if each were a twin
with connections between desires and needs
to enhance a setting of helpful deeds.

Two Cats in Heaven

# A Prayer for Loved Ones in Heaven

Dear Lord,
Our missing loved one's now within your hands,
and peacefully waiting for heavenly plans
when Jesus comes again to rescue all
believers and animals who've heard His call
and want to live with Him in heaven above
forever near family and friends with love.

We believe in heaven as a reality
where we'll forever be joined with family
because we know You are the loving key,
unlocking lives to be with You eternally:

> "In my Father's house there are many dwelling places. If
> it were not so, would I have told you that I go to prepare
> a place for you? And if I go and prepare a place for you, I
> will come again and will take you to myself, so that where
> I am, there you may be also. And you know the way to the
> place where I am going" (John 14: 2–4 NRSV).

Your goodness causes Satan and death to flee
away from our souls, setting us forever free.
You've given to all Christians new lives sin-free
as the bible has referenced for all to see:

> "There is therefore now no condemnation for those who
> are in Christ Jesus. For the law of the Spirit of life in
> Christ Jesus has set you free from the law of sin and of
> death" (Romans 8: 1–2).

Our pets are safe because we know you love
and care for your creations from above.

When Noah was asked to help God with his deeds,
the Lord did save both clean and unclean breeds:

> "Then the Lord said to Noah, 'Go into the ark, you and
> all your household, for I have seen that you alone are
> righteous before me in this generation. Take with you
> seven pairs of all clean animals, the male and its mate;
> and a pair of the animals that are not clean, the male and
> its mate; and seven pairs of the birds of the air also, male
> and female, to keep their kind alive on the face of all the
> earth'" (Gen. 7:1–3 NRSV).

We're thankful, Lord, for all of the joyful times
when we've sung and heard the music of life's rhymes
with friends, family, pets, and yourself above
as you've saved us while sharing goodness and love:

> "Your righteousness is like the mighty mountains,
> your judgments are like the great deep;
> you save humans and animals alike, O Lord" (Psalm 36:6).

Our Christian family's safe within your hands
as you've built forever heavenly lands
for people and animals to share with you
amidst their surprised joy and thanks anew
for all re-connections through eternity
when time with loved ones will rise and never flee.
Amen

# Endnotes

1   Karen Petit, "Preface," *Holidays Amaze* (Bloomington, IN: WestBow Press, 2018), viii.

2   "13th Amendment," 1865, quoted in *history.com,* 2009, accessed July 14, 2019, https://www.history.com/topics/black-history/thirteenth-amendment.

3   "From George Washington to General William Howe, 6 October 1777," *Founders Online,* National Archives, last modified October 5, 2016, https://founders.archives.gov/documents/Washington/03-11-02-0432.

4   Smithsonian Institution, National Museum of American History, Behring Center, "George Washington Sculpture," *si.edu,* https://americanhistory.si.edu/exhibitions/george-washington-sculpture (accessed January 13, 2020).

5   Gaspee Days Committee, Inc., "About The Gaspee Days Committee," *gaspee.com,* 2019, accessed October 11, 2019, http://www.gaspee.com/about.

6   International Spy Museum, "SPYING THAT LAUNCHED A NATION," *spymuseum.org,* 2019, accessed November 8, 2019, https://www.spymuseum.org/exhibition-experiences/gallery-spying-that-shaped-his/.

# About the Author

Dr. Karen Petit (www.drkarenpetit.com) is the author of two books of poetry *(Amazing Holiday Paws* and *Holidays Amaze)* and four novels *(Banking on Dreams, Mayflower Dreams, Roger Williams in an Elevator,* and *Unhidden Pilgrims)*. Petit's books all have dream/reality elements, lots of symbolic content, suspenseful action, historic elements, and photos. This author received her bachelor's, master's, and doctorate degrees in English from the University of Rhode Island. Petit has done many presentations and is a member of the Phi Beta Kappa Society. While attending the University of Rhode Island, she received a second runner-up "Certificate of Achievement" award from the Academy of American Poets.

*Amazing Holiday Paws* is Petit's most recent book of poetry. Maze poems, prayer poems, traditional sonnets, and narratives are all a part of this book. The content about different kinds of animals shows them marching forth through life on their paws. Both animal and human points of view are important components of these poems. The content of this book is enhanced by photos of pets and Washington, D.C.

*Holidays Amaze* was Petit's first published book of poetry. This author had been writing poetry for decades, including poetry for her master's degree in English with a Creative Writing focus. *Holidays Amaze* has content about holidays, as well as a wide variety of poetic structures, pictures, mazes, sonnets, prayer poems, and narratives.

*Banking on Dreams,* Petit's first published book, is a Christian suspense/romance novel about a bank teller who likes ballroom dancing; she uses lucid dreaming techniques to help herself overcome nightmares about a bank vault. The dream/reality connections include the bank teller's past being connected to her present life. When she meets an FBI agent, they soon try to dream the same dream. The Rhode Island setting, ballroom dance scenes, and a bank robbery all add to the interesting content of this novel.

*Mayflower Dreams,* which is historic fiction, has a protagonist who embarks on a real journey and a "dream story" as she explores the history and culture of the Pilgrims. She finds her modern life has connections to the Pilgrims. While fictional, this novel has historically accurate parts, such as quotes from historic figures, the "Mayflower Compact," 107 endnotes, 20 bible quotes, and a "Pilgrim Language" section. Photos from Plymouth tourist attractions are included in this novel.

*Roger Williams in an Elevator,* a Christian suspense novel, has a protagonist who becomes trapped in a partially destroyed building and helps people inside of eight different elevators: yelling, accounting, liberty, watery, fiery, falling, sharing, and hidden. The different elevator communities create their own rules and freedoms. The impact of Roger Williams on our society is seen in this novel's plot, characters, dream/reality connections, symbols, 69 endnotes, 14 bible quotes, and photos of statues, historic items, and the Rhode Island State House.

*Unhidden Pilgrims* is a Christian novel that connects free speech to religious freedom, dreams to reality, and the present to the past with action-filled scenes and pictures of historic items in Providence, Rhode Island, and Plymouth, Massachusetts. The protagonist sometimes has to run, hide, and fight; at other times, she stands her ground, becomes visible, and shares her faith and her love.

Dr. Karen Petit has an author website (www.drkarenpetit.com) with links to her book websites, each of which has a blog:

- an animal blog at *www.amazingholidaypaws.com*
- a holiday blog at *www.holidaysamaze.com*
- a dream blog at *www.bankingondreams.com*
- a "Many Good Thanks" blog at *www.mayflowerdreams.com*
- a freedom blog at *www.rogerwill.com*
- a sharing faith blog at *www.unhiddenpilgrims.com*

Petit loves her family, including her son, daughter, brothers, sisters, aunts, uncle, cousins, nieces, and nephews. As a descendant of the Reverend John Robinson, the pastor to the Pilgrims, Dr. Petit loves to write about history, religious freedom, ancestry, dreams, reality, and our Lord and Savior, Jesus Christ. In addition to writing novels and poetry, Petit has been writing academic documents. She also has been a presenter at multiple libraries and academic conferences, including at the CCCC Conference in 2005 and at the NEWCA Conference in 2013. Some of this author's presentation topics are available on her author website: *www. drkarenpetit.com.*

Dr. Petit not only enjoys writing, but also loves to help other people to write. For more than twelve years, this author has been the full-time Writing Center Coordinator and an adjunct faculty member at the Community College of Rhode Island. Before starting full-time at this college, Petit worked as an adjunct faculty member for over twenty years at many area colleges: Bristol Community College, Massasoit Community College, Rhode Island College, Worcester State University, Quinsigamond Community College, Bryant University, Roger Williams University, New England Institute of Technology, the University of Massachusetts at Dartmouth, and the University of Rhode Island.

Dr. Karen Petit is very thankful for her amazing life. She has been enjoying her author events, as well as a large number of writing and educational activities. Her family, friends, pets, and God have been the focus of her dreams, reality, and amazing holidays for many years.

Printed in the United States
By Bookmasters